STORM OF ATTRACTION

A WILLOWDALE NOVEL

LILY BLACK

Storm of Attraction
The Willowdale Series™
Copyright © 2016 by Lily Black. All rights reserved.
First Print Edition: January 2017

ISBN-13: 978-1-940215-86-0
ISBN-10: 1-940215-86-2

Red Adept Publishing, LLC
104 Bugenfield Court
Garner, NC 27529
http://RedAdeptPublishing.com/

Cover and Formatting: Streetlight Graphics

To my sweet husband, who has shown unfailing faith in me and pushed me to stretch and grow in all the directions I needed to, and also for my son, who was happy to be my punching bag in many a women's self-defense seminar, and to my daughter, who is my biggest fan

CHAPTER ONE

I F ONLY ALL OF LIFE'S problems could be solved by kicking butts or hiding in a book. Alexa was good at both of those. Or she usually was. Today, it would take some deep breaths to feel confident in anything.

She usually loved working two jobs and felt her two "selves" balanced each other out. She shifted from mild-mannered librarian by day to high-kicking black belt instructor by night. But sometimes, coming from a fiasco at her day job—like double-shifting for a sick coworker then spilling the books for the library sale all over the parking lot—could make punching a second time card challenging. Thankfully, it was Friday, and she was on her way to a meeting for all black belt instructors at Crouching Tiger. So she could brighten her day and that of all the other black belts with one quick stop for an icy treat. Black belt buddies plus Crazy Pops equaled win, because the people at Crouching Tiger were like her family, and together they could handle anything.

The gourmet Popsicles were made right there in Willowdale and were a huge favorite with all the locals. Rumor had it that Phyllis, the owner and grande dame who ran Crazy Pops Gourmet Popsicles, enchanted each and every pop so that wishing on the stick would grant the wisher whatever their heart most desired. Of course it was nonsense, but Alexa had found that if she was having a rotten day, she could always trust a quick stop at Crazy Pops to turn her day around.

The door of Crazy Pops Gourmet Popsicles chimed as she pulled it open. She enjoyed how the heels of her black boots thumped on the floor and the way her skirt swirled around her legs as she strode to the counter. No sense in making a bad day worse by being a mouse about it. She smiled at the girl running the register. Alexa managed the older teen programs at the library, and the girl often attended. "Hello, Mandy. What's the special today?"

"You're in luck!" Mandy answered, giving Alexa a big smile. "Today, we have two specials—the spiced pumpkin Ms. Phyllis has brought back for fall, and we also have just a few key lime pops!"

Alexa's stomach dropped into her boots then rolled over and puked. She knew of only one person who had the kind of pull needed to persuade Ms. Phyllis to make key lime pops—her spring treat—in October. But maybe she was wrong. She was having a bad day for luck, and yes, it was Friday, but at least it wasn't the thirteenth. "Key Lime? That's unusual. Any special reason that one's available today?"

Mandy giggled. "Oh, I'd call him a special reason, all right." She tossed her purple hair back and glanced toward Ms. Phyllis's office at the back of the store. Her tone was filled with pride. "Drew Cosimo is putting in a big order. He plans to serve hundreds of Crazy Pops at the grand opening of his new—" She stopped mid-sentence, her mouth still open as her brain finally registered whom she was bragging to.

It took a real effort of will, but Alexa kept her smile firmly fixed in place. "At the grand opening of his new mixed martial arts school? That's a great idea. Bravo to Ms. Phyllis for being able to snag an order like that."

Mandy just stared at her. The poor girl was only sixteen, and as her purple-streaked hair and sweet round face testified, she was far from having all of life's challenges worked out. She snapped her jaw shut. "You'll still order here? You'll still buy your Crazy Pops from us?"

Alexa laughed, the sound only a little rueful. "Where else would I buy them, Mandy? You guys are the only ones!" Mandy didn't look reassured, so Alexa spoke in a rush. "Never mind. Of course I'll still pick up my pops. Let's see... I know Master Hays likes the cookies and cream, and of course we'll need a couple of brownie pops." As she carried on giving her order, Alexa acted cool, calm, and at ease. But inside, her emotions were swirling like a tropical storm well on its way to hurricane status.

Drew was there, right at that moment! She had to hurry and get out of there, and she needed to appear totally calm as she did it. No way was he going to see her running away. It was bad enough that their little rivalry was front-page news, so much so that apparently Mandy thought she would march off in a huff just because Ms. Phyllis was filling an order for Drew.

"I think that will be it." Alexa had ordered enough pops to feed a small army of black belt instructors. "Can I get the pops wrapped up so they won't melt on the way to the dojo?"

Mandy made one last scribble on her order pad. "Sure, let me grab an insulated bag, and we'll get you all set." Her purple hair disappeared behind the counter as she rummaged around.

Alexa was left looking straight through the open door into the small back room. Ms. Phyllis was seated at a table with her planner and an order book open in front of her. Sitting across from her, with his long legs stretched out and a charming smile showing off his dimple, was Drew Cosimo.

He was just as handsome as ever, damn him. Broad shoulders tapered to a lean torso, giving him an air of easy grace, like a warrior prince who'd stepped straight out of the latest swoon-worthy movie. He'd inherited his granddad's dark Italian looks, so it was no wonder she'd fallen hard when he walked into her life five years ago. Tall, dark, and handsome, Drew was every college girl's fantasy. Even knowing what he was, she couldn't help letting her eyes linger on the way his firm, masculine jaw was softened by the gentle smile on his lips.

A memory of those lips fluttered in the back of her mind, but she squashed it instantly. Too bad she couldn't squash the blush as easily.

As if feeling her eyes on him, Drew stirred and glanced toward Alexa.

She gasped and snatched up the flavor chart to hide her face. Mother of Pearl, this was embarrassing. Had he seen her face? And what did she think she was doing, hiding behind a Crazy Pops menu like a lovesick schoolgirl? The Freudians would have a field day with that.

She took a long breath—the force of which made the menu flutter—and let it out slowly. She had a master's degree, and moreover, she had a black belt—second dan—and was an instructor at a martial arts school. In no way was she some fainting female who went into a deep dip just because a dreamy former flame glanced her way. They lived in the same town, so she would just have to get used to run-ins.

Still, another deep breath or two wouldn't hurt. Maybe that would give Drew time to forget she was there.

"Umm," Mandy said from behind Alexa's menu shield. "That's twelve dollars?"

"Right." Alexa shifted the menu to the right just a bit so it still shielded her view into the back room. She spoke quickly, the words tumbling over each other as she pulled out her credit card and passed it to Mandy. "Great menu! Some of these custard flavors look really delicious. I'm going to have to try this lemon-lavender. It sounds heavenly!"

"Would you like me to go ask Ms. Phyllis if she has any in the big freezer?"

"No!" Alexa softened her tone. "No, not today. I've got a meeting at the dojo that I need to get to, but perhaps another time."

In the back office, a chair scraped across the floor, but Alexa kept the menu firmly in place so she wouldn't see—or be seen by—Drew.

Mandy scanned the card, opened the till and closed it, then started printing the receipt. The paper stalled as the machine struggled to feed it properly.

The voices in the back office grew louder. Any minute, they were going to be finished and walk out to the front of the store.

Alexa snatched the bag of pops from the counter. "Don't worry about a receipt," she said in what she hoped was a pleasant voice. "And thanks again!"

Mandy's reply was lost in the dinging of the bell as Alexa escaped out the front of the shop. She stepped quickly around the corner to a little brick-lined lane that led to the parking lot behind the shops, and ducked out of view beside a giant potted plant. She wasn't so much hiding as she was, well, staying out of sight… safe from Drew's perceptive eyes.

She laid her head against the wall behind her and took comfort from the sun-warmed bricks. Leaving without the receipt meant she would be treating the whole staff of Crouching Tiger to ice pops since the rule was no receipt, no refund. But maybe twelve dollars was a bargain if it meant avoiding Drew.

Alexa's lips quirked, and she breathed a laugh. It was a good thing Drew had no idea how desperate she was to avoid him. A cool-headed businessman like him would surely find a way to exploit her distaste. How much would she have to pay him to leave Willowdale entirely? More than she could afford on her small-town librarian's salary, that was certain. Besides, he had enough money, if the fancy, ultra-modern mixed martial arts school and training retreat he was opening was any indication.

The worst part about it all was how embarrassing it was—knowing that everyone was watching their little drama unfold, waiting to see what they would do. Usually, everyone had to read the papers from nearby Raleigh if they wanted to hear about intrigue and broken hearts. The drama between Alexa and Drew was the biggest news their small town had boasted since the big ice storm three years before. She was lucky no one had thought to pop popcorn and pull up a chair.

Of course, she only had herself to blame. She hadn't been discreet over the years, because she never believed Drew would come back. Had she been shortsighted and stupid? Yes. Was that something she could fix now? Not so much. Besides, everything she'd said was true.

However, hiding would not help matters, especially if anyone happened by and wanted to know what had her in a tizzy.

Alexa took a deep breath, glanced right and left, then stepped away from the wall. She walked through the sunny lane to the parking lot. She would simply focus on the present and avoid the trap of what should have been or what might have happened. Today was an easy place to begin. It was a lovely, sunshiny Friday. The air was crisp, with an extra tang to it—like fall's signature wine. The little lane passing from Main Street to the parking lot was an example of all she loved about Willowdale. What could have been a dingy alley was instead a quaint brick garden, complete with giant brass pots overflowing with flowers. How could anyone remain sad in such a setting? A great oak stood tall, spreading its arms out over the parking lot—the crimson of its leaves looked like hundreds of tiny flames flickering against the blue sky.

It had been a while since she'd really looked at that oak, but she'd always loved it. A memory burst into Alexa's mind, sweeping her soul back in time.

It had been late spring, and the leaves on the great oak were a fresh green, while daffodils nodded around its trunk. The night was beautiful, with a fresh breeze and a moon that was almost full. Gibbous, she thought it was called. She'd just finished her junior year in college, and Drew was a newly graduated Ranger. He was on leave, visiting his granddad, who also happened to be the dean of her college. They had only been dating a few days at that point, but their connection was wonderfully intense. Alexa felt special, chosen. She secretly started to wonder what it would be like to someday marry Drew Cosimo, and she enjoyed a delicious tingle at the thought. Never in her life had she fallen for someone the way she tumbled for Drew during that three-week whirlwind romance.

On that lovely evening in the spring, they went to a movie at the little Cineplex at the end of Main. When the movie ended, they took their time walking back to his car. Alexa showed him her favorite haunts and hiding places as a child. When he tried to climb the oak in the dark, he slipped and just barely caught himself from falling. She laughed at him, a Ranger who almost fell on his butt. And he kissed her. Their first kiss was unlike anything she'd experienced before, or since.

Drew certainly knew how to kiss… and that wasn't all he knew. She hadn't been a virgin when they met, but in his hands, she felt like one. The way Drew made love had left her feeling breathless and aware of the world in a new way, as if her senses had been fused with the cosmic connections of the universe and working at perfection.

"Are you wondering where you put your spare tire?" Drew's resonant tenor voice asked from behind her. "Or just searching for patience?"

With a jolt, Alexa came back to reality. Her heart rate zoomed. She turned quickly to face him and took a step back. "What?"

"Your tire." Drew patiently gestured at the driver's side rear tire on her car. "You've got a flat."

Alexa shook her head to clear it then ducked down beside the tire. Why did she always have to blush? Oh, peaches, what if he guessed what she'd been thinking? Of course, she was assuming he even remembered that tree and their first kiss. She shouldn't be too quick to believe their time together had meant anything to him. Heat burned behind her eyes, but thankfully, it was mostly from embarrassment.

Focus, Alexa. Her eyes went to the tire in front of her, and what she saw sobered her up better than an ice cube down the back. It was definitely flat...super flat. Worse, she could just make out a jagged slit in the sidewall. A sick unease settled in her stomach. This tire hadn't gone flat on its own—someone had helped it.

She stood and ignored Drew while she made a quick scan of the nearby cars in the parking lot. No other cars had been messed with. No other tires looked flat. The parking lot was empty, with no likely tire-slashing culprits nearby. It would have been nice if she'd seen some punk teens who might have slashed tires as a prank or college students acting out a misguided initiation. With a sigh, she looked back at the tire, trying to remember who might have been in the parking lot when she had come out of the shop. Had anyone been hanging around? She'd been too caught up in her silly emotions to notice.

Drew shifted closer, seeming to notice her shift in emotions. He waved a hand in a reassuring gesture. "Don't worry, we'll have this changed in no time. Let me run your pops back into the shop so they won't melt. You can clear out the trunk so we can reach the spare."

"I don't—" Alexa stopped herself. She didn't want his help, but she also couldn't quite bring herself to tell him to leave. She'd taught enough self-defense classes to know that this tire problem could be a setup for something more sinister.

She scanned the surrounding cars again. The parking lot looked empty, but what would she do if the person who'd slashed her tire came back to use the knife on her? She couldn't exactly watch her back while changing a tire.

"Come on, Alexa," Drew said. "Surely, you're not going to change this tire by yourself just to spite me? Plus, you're wearing a skirt. Why don't you pretend I'm someone from the library you chatted with in Crazy Pops?"

He held out his hand for the bag. She faced him, ready to tell him no, but his magnetism pulled at her and momentarily sucked the words away. She hated the way her heart tripped over and jolted into a dash as a cocktail of emotions ran through her. First was the inexplicable thrill of pleasure at his closeness. Second was anger at herself, loathing really, for feeling attracted to him despite it all. But that was his gift. He was a real walking, breathing manifestation of the playboy allure. And he was just as likely to settle down and devote himself to one girl.

Drew slipped the bag of Crazy Pops from Alexa's fingers.

She grasped after it, but he was already walking quickly toward the back door of Crazy Pops.

Alexa ground her teeth but let him go. The last thing his ego needed was for her to chase after him. Taking the pops inside was a small thing, and she really didn't want them to melt.

"No way is he changing my tire, though," Alexa muttered. She popped her trunk and started pulling out the thousand and one things that lived in her car—cases of bottled water, a sparring uniform from Crouching Tiger, a *bo* staff, and a box of donated books that she'd already spilled once. She really needed to evaluate them for the library book sale and get them out of her trunk. Everything came out and made a messy pile in the empty parking space beside her car. But Alexa's mind wasn't on her revealing pile of junk; it was on the flat tire.

Why couldn't it be the work of some young vandal, passing through and slashing tires as he went? Sure, that was a long shot, but it was possible, even in Willowdale. Or she might have driven over a sharp branch that had punctured the tire shortly before she parked. Possible, but another explanation was even more likely.

The slashed tire was the work of her stalker, and he had just taken off his kid gloves.

Even as the thought formed in her mind, Alexa shook it out. That was ridiculous, and she wouldn't let herself be paranoid. She'd been down that road before and wasn't going there again. So what if she'd received a few unexplained gifts? In both the library and Crouching Tiger, she worked with kids who might have left her something nice without signing their names. The gifts were probably in no way connected to her tire being slashed. But despite that logic and the warm October sunshine, she couldn't suppress the shiver that ran up her back and raised the hair on her scalp.

A truck pulled up behind her, and Alexa felt her fight instincts go on alert before the guy rolled his window down. Relief left her legs feeling noodly when she saw the friendly face. Stuart Odel was one of the hardest working brown belts at Crouching Tiger, soon to make black belt.

"Got a flat, huh?" he asked. "Need a hand?"

"Yeah, but I'm fine," Alexa said. He was probably on his way to Crouching Tiger, and she didn't want to make him late. The instructors went easier on adults who were late, but it was still frowned on. "The hardest part is digging down to my spare, and I'm near the bottom now."

Stuart chuckled and moved his hand as though he was going to kill the truck and climb out, then his eyes focused on some point behind Alexa, and his face blanched.

Alexa glanced back to see Drew walking toward them, rolling up the sleeves on his blue dress shirt as he walked. She flushed with anger and mentally kicked herself for letting him think he was going to help her in any way. It was obvious Stuart had Drew pegged as her savior, and just as obvious that he wasn't thrilled to see Alexa hanging out with Crouching Tiger's flashy new rival and direct competitor. She knew rumors were flying around the school that Drew could put them out of business. Stuart worked part-time as Crouching Tiger's maintenance guy, so if that were to happen, he would be out of a job she was pretty sure he counted on.

Yet another example of how Drew coming to town made all their lives worse.

Alexa turned back to Stuart with an explanation on her lips, but he was already rolling up his window, his face closed. He gave her a quick nod and pulled away just as Drew reached them.

Alexa let out a breath of air that was almost a curse.

"Sorry, did I chase off a white knight?" Drew smiled as he spoke but eyed the departing truck.

"Of course not," Alexa answered. "Stuart stopped to see if I needed a hand. Which I don't." She flipped up the carpet on the bottom of the trunk and tugged at the spare tire.

"I'm sure that's true," Drew said. "But you're wearing white, and my mother taught me to respect the laundry gods."

Alexa glanced down at her shirt. Her blouse was creamy white and made of a silky material. Below that, her mid-length skirt fluttered above black boots. Definitely not an ideal mechanic's uniform, but at least the sleeves on her blouse could be unbuttoned.

While she tugged at the buttons on her cuffs, Drew reached past her and spun the nut holding the spare tire in place. Then he pulled the donut spare out and reached back in for the jack.

Alexa snatched the jack before he could take it. "Thanks all the same, but I meant what I said. I can change my own tire."

Drew simply nodded and set the donut down. His voice was casual. "Better to change it yourself than accept a hand from the devil, right?" He tilted his head slightly as he met her eyes. His were deep brown and held humor as well as some other emotion that she couldn't read. He quirked one eyebrow. "After all, you can't have it get around the dojo that you're fraternizing with the enemy, a money-grubbing bastard with no respect for tradition and no real knowledge of the ancient martial arts."

Alexa felt her jaw drop and heat flash into her cheeks. She'd called him those things along with a few other insults. She'd been very angry at his flashy talk of "real-world martial arts" and "effective self-defense." She doubted he was ignorant regarding what his words implied about Crouching Tiger—and everything that Crouching Tiger wasn't. But she hadn't thought he would hear her rantings.

Okay, so maybe she'd let her mouth run on, but it had only been with one or two close friends… and her black belt buddies… and her fellow librarians.

Drew, taking advantage of her surprise, removed the jack from her hands and fit it under the frame of her car.

"I'm not complaining," he said. "With our history, all the drama and name-calling has generated interest in my studio. Not all of it good, of course. But enough people have come to me with questions that I've been able to clarify what mixed martial arts is all about." He flashed her a grin that was one part charming, two parts teasing. "I expect to have a good turnout for my grand opening next week."

Alexa grabbed the lug nut wrench and waved it around a little wildly. "Well, isn't that great? You can show them all the nifty moves you learned as a Ranger and maybe outfit them with an AK-47. Or would you rather show them how to climb a sheer cliff while making a picnic lunch?"

She'd meant it mockingly, but instead it came out sounding almost like admiration. Which only annoyed her further. She stomped over to the flat tire and crouched beside it, straining to loosen the lug nuts. If she could just get them started, the rest would be easy.

Drew's silence while she pulled only made her yank harder, but the bolts absolutely refused to budge. She could probably break them loose if she jumped on the lug wrench, but in her skirt and boots, she wasn't sure she could keep her balance. What if she fell in front of Drew? Or worse, what if she fell *into* Drew?

He glanced back at the store. "It looks like the store might be closing—you know Ms. Phyllis and her odd hours. Maybe you'd better pick up your Crazy Pops before she locks up?"

Alexa could hear his unspoken offer. She could save face by picking up the pops, and he would get the tire changed before she came back. She didn't know which was worse—that she was going to have to let him change the tire or that he felt the need to protect her dignity.

She dropped the wrench without a word and marched back to Crazy Pops to rescue the bag of treats. As she opened the shop door, she looked back at Drew, who was busily changing her tire. She shook her head. There was no understanding that man.

He hadn't said boo to her when he moved back to Willowdale, hadn't even asked her out for coffee, let alone apologized for how he'd treated her five years ago. Was it any wonder she hadn't welcomed him and his MMA school? The whole thing made her blood boil. He was the last person she would call a friend. Yet there he was, helping her out as if they were best buddies.

And what had he meant by "our history"? Just how did he view that little episode in their past? A three-week fling? Crazy summer love?

Five years ago, she had fallen deeply in love with Drew, and at the time, she believed he felt the same. She'd thought it was one of those incredible romances that blossomed overnight because true love couldn't be denied. As she grew more experienced, she realized just how naive her little crush had been and how Drew must have viewed her as totally insignificant. Sure, the sex had been fantastic, and Drew had been a thoughtful and attentive boyfriend, but he wasn't the staying type. It had just been a pleasant way for him to spend his leave before he got back to his real life in the army. In the years since, he'd probably charmed his way through dozens of weeks of leave, making each girl feel cherished for just as long as he was there.

In the end, Alexa had been left to regret the strength of her own feelings. And she had kept on regretting them through every relationship since. Better to be alone and bitter, though, than to ever admit how badly she'd fallen for the darling playboy.

She would never expose herself to that kind of pain again. If he wanted a polite—and false—friendship, two could play that game.

Inside Crazy Pops, Mandy took one look at Alexa's face, and her eager grin faltered. "Oh, I thought—Drew said you had a flat, so um..." She trailed off, her eyes confused.

Obviously, she'd thought that all it would take for Drew and Alexa to fall madly in love once again was a flat tire and a few moments of his muscles bulging as he changed it.

Alexa bit back a groan and made her voice pleasant. "Yes, I had a flat tire, but thankfully, I'm ready to go again. Could I have my pops, please?" She knew she was telling a lie of omission by ignoring the fact that Drew was back there changing her tire, but she simply couldn't stomach a single word of Mandy's girlish speculation.

Mandy seemed to sense her mood and was quick to get the bag of pops and wish Alexa a nice afternoon. But Alexa's conscience was already bothering her.

"I'd also like—that is, could you add a kiwi and fruit pop to my order?"

Mandy's eyes lit up. "Oh, yes, of course! Good thinking." She rang up the pop and handed it over, smiling at Alexa as if they shared a secret.

Alexa endured it because she'd done more than her share of grumping this afternoon already.

Let Mandy think whatever schoolgirl fantasies will make her heart happy. Alexa saw picking up the extra pop as her way of paying Drew back for changing her tire, so she wouldn't feel indebted to him. She schooled her features into a pleasantly polite look as she walked back to her car. That same look was usually reserved for old Mr. Rine, a patron of the library who had a reputation for being difficult.

Alexa kept the bland smile in place as she approached, even when Drew glanced up and seemed to look appreciative before glancing away. It was kind of nice, actually, to know she still looked good to him. *Let him savor a little regret.*

She breezed past him and set the bag of treats on the passenger seat of her car. Taking out the pop she'd bought for Drew, she shut the car door just as he put the jack back into the trunk.

"You missed your calling in life," Alexa said as she came up beside him. "You should have worked in a NASCAR pit."

Drew chuckled. "Only if the driver was a beautiful woman."

She took a half step back, not sure if she felt more flustered at the implied compliment or more disgusted that he seemed to be confirming her opinion of him as a playboy. Giving her head a tiny shake, she held out the pop to him. "I picked this up for you. My way of saying thank you." It didn't come out as smoothly as she would have liked, but it was the best she could do.

"Thanks. That'll just hit the spot." Drew wiped his hands on a scrap of cloth before he reached for the pop. His deep-brown eyes met hers in that intense way he had before glancing down at the pop. His hand hesitated for just a fraction of a second.

Alexa frowned. What was wrong with it? Why didn't he just take it? She looked at the pop, too, and felt a furious blush flash up into her cheeks. She'd intended to buy him a random flavor without giving it any thought. Apparently, she'd bought kiwi-passion fruit, the pop the two of them used to call the "kissing pop" because it made for great kisses afterward.

She dropped the pop as though it had suddenly sprouted legs and turned into a spider.

Drew caught it, cradling it in his hand as his long fingers cupped around it.

Alexa took another step back. Her polite smile was long gone, and her breath was coming fast. She bent and began furiously tumbling her mess of stuff back into the trunk. Her words came out in a rapid fire. "Thank you, again. Very nice of you. Now I'm off to class. Best get all this stuff cleaned up so I won't be late."

She threw the bo staff in last on top of the rest the mess and turned once again to face Drew. Her hand was on the trunk, ready to slam it shut.

He was rolling her flat tire over to his truck. He gave her a ready smile as he tossed it in the back. "This tire won't fit in the pocket left by your spare, so no point in trying to fit it in. Tell me where you want it repaired, and I'll drop it off for you."

Alexa groaned inside. Letting him take her tire would mean he would be doing yet another nice thing for her, but the alternative was unpacking everything from her trunk in front of him again, while he sucked down his passion pop. That made the decision easy, really. "Handy Man Auto and Tire, if it's not out of your way."

Drew nodded. Was it just her imagination, or did his grin look a little too happy about her choice of Handy Man's?

"Thank you again for changing the tire," she said stiffly, trying to get them back on professional footing. "I'm happy to return the favor any time." Return the favor? Right, like he was going to need her help getting his tire changed.

"No problem. Happy to help." Drew held out his hand—which he'd cleaned off—for her to shake.

Reluctantly, Alexa extended her hand. She normally hated wimpy, fingertip handshakes, but today, that was all she was willing to offer.

Their fingers touched, palms hovering a breath apart. It felt like a splash of rain on parched, dry earth.

Drew's fingers wrapped around hers, cradling her hand like a man holds his lover. She couldn't stop the tremor that ran through her fingers.

Drew cleared his throat. "Alexa, is this enmity necessary? We both have a passion for martial arts. My mixed martial arts school could be an asset, a real support to Crouching Tiger, if you'd give it a chance."

Alexa jerked her fingers free as if they'd touched a live socket. "Crouching Tiger doesn't need your support and doesn't want it."

Drew held up his hand, asking for her to wait. "I'm not saying Crouching Tiger needs my help. But we could be stronger working together. I'll be stopping by your school to see if Master Hays would be willing to offer a demonstration from Crouching Tiger students at my grand opening. I'd appreciate having you back me up."

Alexa couldn't believe her ears. Was he truly going to bargain her school in exchange for his help with her tire? He was asking for her support because she'd offered to—oh, it was too much. No words came out of her mouth, but sometimes, words weren't needed. She whirled around and jumped into the driver's seat of her car then drove away without a backward glance.

From the hot flush that made her face tight and her ears ring, she couldn't tell if she was more mortified or angry. She should be grateful, because for just a second, she had been influenced by his charm, his looks, and the way her every pore seemed to open up when he was close. It was a very good thing he'd reminded her what kind of man he really was—the kind who didn't stand a chance with her.

CHAPTER TWO

ALEXA PARKED HER CAR A little ways down from Crouching Tiger, tucking it behind a big van so there was no chance anyone in the dojo would see the spare tire. It wasn't that she was ashamed she'd let Drew help her change it—she just wasn't in the mood to discuss it, so she would rather avoid questions. In a town like Willowdale, word was sure to get out, but hopefully this would buy her time.

With the bag of Crazy Pops swishing in her hand, Alexa broke into a skimming jog that accommodated her skirt and cut across the parking lot to the sidewalk.

"You don't have to run," her friend Keri called from up ahead. "We know about your flat, so we put the meeting on hold 'til you got here."

"Oh… great." Alexa slowed to a walk and eyed her friend. With her sleek black hair pulled back into a ponytail, and her willowy figure dressed in the white martial arts uniform, Keri looked like an advertisement in Martial Arts Monthly. But how had they heard about the flat? And more importantly, did they know who'd helped her?

Keri fell into step with Alexa and leaned in. She lowered her voice to a conspiratorial whisper. "So, what caused the flat? Could you tell?"

Alexa's gut clenched, and she gave thanks that her stomach was empty. She'd been so worried about Drew and what people would think of him helping her that she'd managed to put the ugly slit in the tire sidewall out of her mind.

"Your face tells me all I need to know," Keri said. "It was slashed, right? Have you told the police?"

"No, but I will talk to Master Hays, see what he suggests." Alexa stepped past Keri and opened the door to the school, hoping that would end the discussion. She knew Keri didn't understand her reluctance to go to the police, and she wasn't sure she understood it herself. She just knew—from painful experience—that getting the police involved meant paperwork, questions, and a willingness to let them examine every private detail of her life.

"Alexa." Keri tugged her into the meeting room on the side of the lobby and shut the door. "I don't want to badger you about this or upset you, but you've helped me teach the women's self-defense class. What is it we always tell them? The sooner you talk to the police, the sooner they can start collecting evidence and building a case about this guy. The number one mistake women make is keeping a stalker situation to themselves and trying to handle it alone."

Alexa sighed and sank into the nearest chair. "Right. I know. But how can the police do anything when I don't know who it is? There's no evidence, no face. I'll contact them as soon as I feel they can help, okay?"

Keri looked mutinous, but the room was filling up with their fellow black belt instructors, so she let it drop, for which Alexa was grateful. Someday, she was going to have to tell her friend about the violent assault she'd witnessed her last year of college and the months of paranoid fears and panic attacks that had followed. *Someday, but not today.*

As the instructors settled around her, Alexa passed out the Crazy Pops and nibbled quietly on her own Mexican chocolate. Brian grabbed Keri's attention, asking if she'd seen the latest episode in a show they were both watching.

Then Master Hays arrived and started the meeting. He wanted to discuss a tournament Crouching Tiger had been invited to, which was several months out but sounded like a good experience for the students.

Alexa tried to keep her mind on the meeting, but she found her thoughts wandering back to the slash in her tire. She couldn't shake the sick feeling that had formed in the pit of her stomach the moment she had seen the ragged cut.

She would feel better when this meeting was over and she could get on with teaching. She would feel even better once she got a bit of sparring in tonight. She needed to make sure she was paired with a fellow black belt, because she didn't feel like holding back.

When the meeting was over, she caught Master Hays's eye and signaled that she would like him to stay for a minute.

Master Hays nodded and waited quietly while the room emptied. Alexa watched him, thinking how well he embodied the silent and serene sensei, with his silver hair and wise eyes. But she knew he was also a man of experience in the world, and she was tapping into that side now. She trusted his judgment and wanted his insights on her stalker problem, and as an added bonus, coming to Master Hays would sooth Keri's concerns.

When the last black belt filed out, Alexa took a deep breath. She spoke quickly so she wouldn't chicken out. "I have a stalker. He slashed my tire today."

Master Hays's eyebrows rose, and he leaned forward. "Is this person someone you know?"

She shook her head and related what had happened so far. She left out the part where Drew had helped her change her tire. Master Hays probably already knew, but if he didn't, she wasn't going to tell him.

"I see." The sensei leaned back, his eyes resting on Alexa's face. "And you do not wish to involve the police as yet. Because they might take your concerns as the paranoid ranting of an overwrought female?"

Alexa nodded, grateful he understood. She had discussed her issues with him—her PTSD symptoms from an incident three years ago—when she'd first started learning self-defense and was having a hard time handling the physical closeness and calm it required. "Besides, what can they do at this point? They don't have the manpower to give me a guard, and they have nothing to go on in catching this guy."

"Perhaps you should give them more credit, Alexa." He leaned forward and tucked her hand into his. His voice was gentle. "You are known here and will not be lightly dismissed. If anything further happens, promise me you will involve the police."

She nodded, relieved he wasn't insisting on it just yet.

Master Hays sat back. "I had hoped you wished to speak of our young competitor, that perhaps your feelings toward him had softened after his help this afternoon."

Alexa felt a quick flush rise in her cheeks and took a calming breath in hopes she could force the tattletale pink back down. "You've heard the things he says about Crouching Tiger, about traditional martial arts. One good deed doesn't erase all that."

Master Hays nodded. "That is true, but much of what he says about our school is also true." He smiled slightly at Alexa's shocked face. "We cater to young children, who cannot hope to compete with an adult fighter, no matter how well they learn their kata. We offer classes that are geared toward fitness, not fighting, and take all comers, regardless of their athleticism. We also don't pretend to train all or most of our students into fighters who can take the kind of beating dished out in a mixed martial arts ring."

"So what if MMA manages to pound some skills into their fighters?" Alexa asked. "You can say that of any gang on the street too. Where are the values, the respect? Where is the rising generation that understands its place in a balanced world?" She made a flicking motion with her fingers as if tossing garbage to the curb. "Drew can jump on the MMA fad and ride it right out of town. He'll never convince me that it has any lasting worth."

Master Hays smiled but shook his head at her. "We are always open to learning, Alexa. New things do not threaten the old unless tradition is abandoned. Drew called a few minutes ago, and I invited him here this afternoon to witness our brick-breaking demonstration. Who knows, it may begin a positive relationship between our schools. We have much to teach each other."

"Oh, fabulous." Alexa shoved the chair back as she stood. "Let's start a 'symbiotic' relationship in which Drew stomps all over traditional martial arts and buys us out when we're thoroughly flattened."

Master Hays lifted his hand. "I understand you don't like it. However, he'll be our guest while he's here, and I would appreciate it if you could set an example for the other black belts in civility." He leaned forward again. "Alexa, I knew Drew's father and grandfather. I knew him as a boy and watched him through the years when he came back to visit his grandfather. I saw him grow to be a man. I trust him."

Alexa wondered if that extended to trusting Drew's cutthroat business sense, but she swallowed her retort and nodded. "I'll be civil."

Master Hays smiled and got to his feet. "Good. With my lovely Joanne and myself out of town for the next few days, I'll rest easier if I know you won't start a war while we're away."

"No wars, but I may not be able to prevent a skirmish or two," Alexa said with a laugh. They walked together to the door leading out into the lobby. "Where will the two of you be going? The ocean or the mountains?"

"We still haven't decided," Master Hays answered with tranquil satisfaction. "It is our plan to tumble along like the windblown leaves."

Alexa laughed again, enjoying the thought. Mrs. Hays, "the lovely Joanne," was as sweet and grandmotherly as anyone could wish, but she also had a whimsical streak that asserted itself once in a while and took absolute control over Master Hays's more practical side. In the face of a stalker and painful memories, Alexa felt good knowing that love endured and sweetened life.

She smiled at the students gathered in the lobby. The class of eight- through eleven-year-olds was at full chatter, hotly debating what kind of pie was best. They broke off when she walked in, and chorused a greeting.

"Is it time to line up, Ms. Wolving?" Brianna was an eleven-year-old bundle of energy with terrific kicks and a quick smile.

"What, and me teach class in my skirt?" Alexa asked in mock horror. The kids all laughed, and Brianna smacked both hands across her face in comic dismay at her goof.

"Don't worry, I'll change quickly. And when it's time to line up, you can lead the bows," Alexa told her. Brianna was all smiles again, so Alexa left the group and slipped into the changing room for a quick wardrobe swap. Out with the sweet, flower-attired librarian, in with the kick-butt black belt. That thought always amused her. As the heavy fabric of her *gi* settled over her shoulders, she felt her general agitation from the day disappear. Replacing it was the energized calm she enjoyed in the dojo.

This was her sanctuary, her refuge, and her release. As she stopped in the doorway of the dojo and bowed, she embraced the feeling and smiled.

Brianna led the class in lining up and did a superb job leading them through the bow and oath. Alexa nodded to herself, pleased at the young girl's progress. When she first joined Crouching Tiger, she had been so shy that no one could hear her when she whispered that she needed to go to the bathroom. Now she was capable of giving the whole class commands.

Alexa accepted the students' bows to her then turned the group over to the teenage black belts, who led them through their kata. They started with the white belt form and worked on up.

Alexa walked the edges of the group, nodding her approval. There were occasional fumbles, especially among the white and yellow belts, but for the most part, the class was moving in sync. Even more impressive, they were getting their breathing right, and the upper belts moved with the calm grace of a true martial artist in the zone.

Alexa enjoyed a swell of satisfaction and almost maternal pride in her students as spunky Morgan stood on tiptoe and stretched her arms wide to execute the slow-breathing rest just before the end of the brown belt form. Next to her, Jake looked a little less poised. His rangy body didn't take well to tiptoeing, but he was still pulling it off. Then Jake and Morgan came out of the slow rest and flashed through the end of the form, landing the final jump perfectly in sync.

Alexa grinned and moved forward to congratulate the kids on a job well done. The neo martial artists like Drew could mock the kata all they wished. She knew the forms served a useful place in martial arts training. The kata taught breathing, control, and instinctive understanding of one's environment, all while cementing the basic moves that made up a martial artist's repertoire. Drew could keep his souped-up street smarts. She would stick to the time-honored traditions of the age-old martial arts, thanks all the same.

The rest of the class was spent teaching the students their belt-appropriate combinations. Several kids received a new stripe on their belt, which was always something that made their eyes sparkle. The class bowed out, and Alexa bowed out of the dojo with them, intent on grabbing a sip of water before she was needed for the breaking demonstration.

Keri intercepted her on her way to the water cooler. Eyes alive with eagerness, Keri leaned in and kept her voice to a whisper. "I just heard who helped you change your tire. Why didn't you tell me? Or better yet," she added with a laugh, "text me so I could come and watch the fireworks?"

Alexa shushed Keri, her eyes darting to see who had heard. Her friend's whisper carried easily in the hallway, and the students were watching them. But she wondered why she hadn't texted Keri. Or better yet, why hadn't she called her friend? If she'd whipped out her phone the minute she knew her tire was flat, Keri could've been there in time to help her with the stubborn lug nuts and Drew would've had no reason to stick around. Was there some Freudian part of her that had *wanted* Drew's help? *No way.*

She thrust that thought away as soon as it flashed through her brain. So she wasn't immune to the effects of his charisma. So what? She knew better than to throw herself at a heartbreaker. No way was she that pathetic.

She looked back at Keri and sighed at the speculative look in her friend's eyes. That was one thought she would have to nip in the bud. "I planned to go get a snack after the breaking class, before I come back for the sparring class. If you want to get coffee with me, and you promise not to say a word until we're safely away from the dojo and in no danger of being overheard, I'll tell you every single detail."

Keri laughed and gave Alexa a half hug. "So long as the details are sordid and the coffee is strong."

Alexa hugged her friend back and refrained from making an *ugh* face.

Drew paused on the sidewalk to read the announcements taped to the glass beside the front door of Crouching Tiger. Testing was in two weeks, so pre-tests would be some time in the next week. A party for all belt levels was scheduled for later in the month and would include a movie and video games for the kids, while parents had a night out.

He shook his head. That was another reason why his studio would keep its focus on the practical application of mixed martial arts and real-life self-defense situations. As much as he loved kids, he didn't think it was his job as an instructor to be their babysitter. Besides, it wasn't as if he could pass on his skills as a trained combat veteran and Ranger to a pack of little kids. At best, the youth programs like the one offered by Crouching Tiger gave kids a sense of self and a desire to learn. At worst, the pseudo fighting and fancy moves left kids with an inflated sense of their own abilities and turned them into egotistical bullies.

Alexa had accused him of being a money-grubbing pretender, but he was willing to bet Crouching Tiger made most of their cash from the youth programs.

Still, he respected Master Hays and was quite willing to support his team in offering their brand of martial arts, while he offered his. Maybe Drew's visit would help foster the goodwill needed for such an arrangement—Alexa or no Alexa.

He opened the door and stepped inside the spacious lobby. To his left were a small office and a storage room. To his right were a closed door and an impressive wall of trophies. Through the big glass windows in front, he could see a class in progress.

Little kids ran around the lobby and played on the floor, so Drew stepped carefully as he walked through.

"Look, they're starting the breaking!" a boy of maybe six called out. His little sister had been sprawled on the floor. She jumped up and charged over to the windows, squirming between the other watchers to get a good view.

Drew had to smile. Okay, maybe if he had the chance to have kids one day, he would want them to have a place like Crouching Tiger where they could train.

He stopped in the doorway to the dojo and slipped off his shoes before entering. The students were gathered in the dojo center, so he made his way toward them. The rail behind him, the mirrors on the wall across from him, and the slight give of the mats under his feet reminded him of the little bit of traditional martial arts training he'd had as a boy.

As he entered, he could hear Master Hays discussing the technique involved in breaking brick. Then Alexa's voice took over the instruction. Drew stopped at the outer edge of the circle of students, where he could look among them and watch unobtrusively.

Alexa stood on the far side of the group, facing Drew and the biggest cluster of students. In front of her, a smooth surface had been laid down on the mat floor, and bricks were set up on it. Two fat cinder blocks stood on their ends and provided upright supports on which a third cinder block rested. As Alexa talked, she stepped forward and placed one foot beside the standing brick on her left, and Drew saw the whole getup wobble. Alexa steadied the blocks, seemingly without giving it any thought, and continued to explain to the gathered students the principal points of a clean break.

"Remember to turn your hand to the side," she said. "So it's aligned with the brick, then hit it with the thickest part of your palm. Anybody want to tell me why we hit with that part of the palm?"

A smiling teen with her hair pulled into a ponytail raised her hand. "Because that's the strongest part of the palm?"

"Yes, but also because hitting with that part of the palm allows you to provide the most impact in the smallest space." As Alexa spoke, several students held their own hands up, looking at their palms as if seeing them for the first time.

"You want to shock the brick, send all the force of your energy through it," Alexa said. "Simply slapping it will only make your hand hurt, and punching it will cause the energy to travel back up your arm." She gave the students a grin. "Very painful, that. If you're lucky, you'll just jump around and swear. If you're unlucky, your arm will hurt for upwards of a week. With the right technique, your hand will go through the brick like it's slicing butter."

As she finished, Alexa's upper body was centered directly over the brick. She lifted up on her toes then dropped her center of gravity, while bringing the heel of her palm down on the brick in a sharp motion—down, then up. The brick sliced cleanly in two and clattered to the floor.

A scattering of applause came from the group of students and instructors.

Alexa stepped back, and a black belt standing by cleared away the broken halves of the brick then put another cinder block in its place. Drew couldn't help noticing that the black belt was a good-looking guy who probably got plenty of attention from the girls. The guy was built like a tank and worked comfortably side by side with Alexa. Was it just Drew's imagination, or did the guy seem to watch Alexa a little possessively when he stepped back?

Ugh. Maybe they were dating. Drew caught himself wondering how many push-ups the other guy could do and if he could keep military form while he did them. He quickly reined in his thoughts. If Alexa liked that kind of guy, there was nothing he could do about it—and given that he only wanted a working business relationship, he shouldn't have even noticed the competition.

"Remember, you want to drop your center of gravity as you break," Alexa said. "Try to coordinate the movement so you hit the brick at the bottom of your drop. Let your body's movement help you and keep the drop clean and quick." She rose up a bit, preparing to drop into the move, and Drew shifted so he could get a better view.

Alexa's eyes met his just as she dropped into the move. Even from across the room and with an untutored eye, Drew could see she hit the brick a lot harder than she had the last one.

The cinder blocks rocked. The top brick broke, and the two supporting blocks toppled over.

Drew stepped forward—an impulsive gesture, since he wasn't nearly close enough to help.

Alexa snatched her foot back, but she'd waited too long. The cinder blocks slammed down on her foot.

Her face contorted with pain. "Fiddlesticks," she ground out.

A tall female black belt jumped forward to support Alexa by the arm. Alexa accepted the support but gave her students a grim smile. "That was an example of excessive force, and it also demonstrates why you move your foot back out of the way after each break." She looked to Master Hays, and some signal passed between them. "Brian." She nodded to the black-belt stud who'd helped set up the bricks. "Could you take charge here and let the conditional belts start breaking?"

Brian nodded and moved forward to set up the cinder blocks. Alexa leaned on the arm of her friend and made her way across the dojo toward the lobby.

Drew told himself he wasn't needed, that Alexa was in the hands of her friend. But he couldn't pretend her accident wasn't his fault. She'd been looking right at him when the bricks fell.

He waited while two conditional belts attempted to break, neither having any luck. When the third student managed to crunch through the brick, Drew used the cover of general applause and high fives to follow Alexa.

As he entered the lobby, he heard low laughter and what sounded like a smothered giggle from the storage room. He went to the door and rapped at the frame with his knuckles before looking in.

Alexa was seated on a barstool pulled up next to a small sink. Her foot was extended, and her friend was patting it dry. Both of them looked up at Drew with surprise on their faces.

"I, uhm…" Drew cleared his throat. "I wanted to see how your foot is. I'm sorry you got hurt."

"Thanks, but it's not your fault, and also not the first time I've forgotten to pull my foot free," Alexa said.

Her friend's head was bent over the bloody scrapes on the top of Alexa's foot, but Drew heard her murmured response. "Yeah, just the first time you've hit the brick that hard."

Alexa gave her friend a not-so-subtle jab, which only confirmed Drew's suspicion that she'd messed up her break because of him.

"It's just some surface bleeding and a bit of bruising," Alexa said, as if making an effort to be polite. "We're only bandaging it so I won't get blood on my white gi."

Her friend dabbed ointment on the cuts then wound gauze around Alexa's foot and reached for the scissors.

"Here, let me." Drew stepped forward and picked up the scissors. Cutting the gauze one-handed would have been awkward.

"No, that's fine, thanks." Alexa quickly reached out and took the scissors from him. "Keri and I are quite capable of getting this patched up, and I'm sure Master Hays would prefer it if you were out there where you belong."

Those last three words seemed to slip out, and Alexa's face showed her surprise that they'd been spoken aloud.

Drew resisted the urge to snap off a sharp comeback. The woman really was too stubborn for words. He folded his arms across his chest and tried to speak pleasantly. "Sorry to bother you. I felt responsible, so I—"

"Responsible?" Alexa's hazel eyes pinned him with a look that implied he was the world's biggest moron. "For what? My hyper-enthusiasm and slow reflexes? How could you possibly be responsible?"

Drew made an exasperated sound. "You looked at me—"

Alexa laughed. "Yeah, and I looked at almost everyone else in the dojo too. Try not to get a big head about it." She turned away from him, dismissing him with her posture. Her friend held the gauze, and Alexa snipped it, then held it in place while her friend dug out the tape. Neither of them looked at Drew.

He turned on his heel and walked out, but he didn't miss the sound of laughter that erupted just as soon as he was gone. A quick roll of his head dismissed their laughter, and he pushed open the front door. He would catch up with Master Hays later and let him know the brick-breaking class had been very impressive. But at that moment, he needed to put some space between him and Alexa before he decided to try shaking some sense into her. As a Ranger, he'd been in some tricky situations. Missions had dropped him down behind enemy lines with ten men under him and a hostage to extract. But none of that compared to the absolute impossibility of understanding Alexa Wolving.

CHAPTER THREE

ALEXA HOBBLED HER WAY THROUGH the rest of the breaking class, but it was obvious she wouldn't be sparring that night. Not at her usual level, anyway. Which was too bad. She'd wanted to go a round with Stuart. She owed him some one-on-one time if he was going to be ready for his black belt test. As an adult student, he'd struggled to find the right balance between force and finesse, and Master Hays was keeping him at brown until he learned it. If she was honest with herself, though, she had another reason she was interested in talking with Stuart. She wanted to make sure he understood that Drew's coming to the breaking class hadn't been her idea. After he saw Drew helping her with the flat tire, he might wonder, and that was one bit of gossip she would like to nip in the bud before it even started.

Unfortunately, Master Hays caught her flinching when she put too much weight on her foot and ordered her out of her gi and into her street clothes. Keri followed her after having a quick word with Master Hays.

"I'm to take you down the block to Marcellino's and get you some comfort food," she said. "After that, I'll drive you home and see to it you take some pain meds before going to bed."

Alexa scoffed. "As if. It's not that bad. It just smarts where the raw spots keep sticking to the underside of the bandage. Pain meds will not be needed, though I won't say no to some comfort food. And no way are you driving me home. First, 'cause I need my car and the stuff in it for morning. And second, 'cause I've seen the way you drive."

Keri laughed. "Fine, but let me treat you to dinner and carry your stuff to your car." She said it as though it was already settled and smiled quietly as she helped Alexa hang up her gi.

Alexa tilted her head. "You knew I wouldn't let you drive me home, didn't you? That was just a ploy, so I'd let you baby me between now and then."

Keri smiled as she raised her hands in surrender. "Is it my fault you're so stubbornly independent that you won't accept help without your friends resorting to trickery?"

Alexa sputtered a protest and followed Keri out the dojo door.

Keri shook her head. "Your friends know you too well. Brian tried to bet me earlier that by the end of the breaking class, or sparring at the latest, your frustration with Drew would make you overdo it, and you'd be hurt."

"You guys bet on that?" Alexa asked, outraged. She forgot to hobble for a couple of steps, and the pain in her foot reminded her to go easy. It was a good thing Marcellino's was so close by.

"No, he tried to bet me." Keri waved thanks to a car that let them cross the side street between their school and the restaurant. "I wouldn't put any money down, 'cause I was sure he was right."

Alexa laughed. "Remind me to consult the two of you next time I need the advice of a psychic."

They were still laughing when Keri pulled open the door to Marcellino's. They let the hostess lead them to a patio table since it was a nice night. The tables were surrounded by a screen of shrubs and flowers, and the outdoor seating space was lit by tiny sparkling white lights. Thankfully, there were several larger parties seated on the patio, so Alexa and Keri weren't the only ones dining sans dates.

Keri was true to her promise that she wouldn't ask about Drew until no one was listening, and didn't mention Drew or the tire change all through ordering and the arrival of the soft homemade Italian bread Marcellino's was famous for. Instead, they talked about Keri's latest art projects and the painted glass show she had coming up in a few weeks at the gallery.

But as soon as the server had left the appetizer they planned to share—they'd decided against a full dinner since Alexa wasn't that hungry and Keri still had sparring class—Keri leaned forward. "All right now, spill. How did it come about that you let Drew change your tire?"

Alexa smiled faintly, appreciating her friend's wording. How had it come about that she let Drew change her tire? "I was trying to be super cool with things. Deflate the rumors that have spread about us." She launched into a description of her conversation with Mandy and the girl's assumption that Alexa would storm out of Crazy Pops once she knew Drew was placing a big order with them.

Keri nodded in sympathy, demonstrating her worth as a friend all over again. Of course it was Alexa's own fault that people thought she hated Drew, but Keri was kind enough not to mention that.

"When I realized Drew could come out any minute, and moreover, that the menu was sadly insufficient as a long-term hiding place," Alexa continued, "I made a dash for the exit and the parking lot."

Keri set her glass down with a clink of ice. "That's why we didn't have to pay for our pops! You didn't get the receipt."

Alexa straightened in her chair and put on a dramatic air. "What are receipts and mundane money details to a girl who is desperately trying to avoid a boy?"

Keri laughed. "Nothing, of course. Women of principle and heart can feast on their convictions and clothe themselves with the finery of righteous scorn."

"There you go!" Alexa tossed her hands in the air. "Unfortunately, they can't fix a slashed tire and apparently need help changing it."

Keri nodded, sobering, but she seemed to sense Alexa's preference that they not dwell on the stalker, so moved past that topic. "So, describe the scene for me. Did he take off his shirt? Remember, I've dated very little of late, and give me every detail!"

Alexa sputtered. "No, he did not take off his shirt! Don't you dare let that turn into a rumor. I'll have enough to live down, as is." She went on to describe the discomfort of the tire change—complete with heated moments whenever their hands touched—in dramatically lurid tones. Keri was laughing so hard at the story that she nearly snorted her mushrooms.

Twenty minutes and a delicious plate of bruschetta later, Alexa sat back and sipped her espresso. "So I told Drew he could forget my helping him get in Crouching Tiger's good graces—not that he needed my help, it seems. Then I piled into my car and left." She watched Keri as her friend looked thoughtfully into her macchiato.

Keri straightened and fixed Alexa with a serious look. "Do you still love him?"

"What?" Alexa sputtered, spraying coffee on her chin. "No! Of course not." She grabbed a napkin.

Keri went on. "Because I think he might feel something for you. All joking aside, the most gallant suitor or romantic gentleman couldn't have been more considerate of your feelings. While I'm sure Drew Cosimo is as thoughtful as they come, I doubt he'd be that way for just anyone. And that's before we add in his schoolboy nerves when he stopped by to check on your foot. I mean, he's a Ranger! But you wouldn't know it from the way you sent him packing." She gave Alexa a mischievous smile. "So would your answer still be no if you thought he returned your feelings?"

"Keri, that's just..." Alexa shook her head. Her fingers twisted the napkin into something roughly resembling a unicorn horn. "What Drew feels, or doesn't feel, would make no difference. We had our chance five years ago. If he cared about me, he would have returned my calls, kept in touch. More importantly, he wouldn't have acted like a jerk and then blown me off without taking the chance to make things right or at least end things well. He didn't, and that opportunity has passed."

"So, you do care about him," Keri said softly.

"No... or yes." Alexa held up a hand to forestall Keri. "But only as a man I once loved during a lovely summer in my past. The here-and-now Drew, I don't care for at all. Moreover, there is absolutely no chance I will ever let Drew back into my heart, no matter what twists life throws at me."

Keri pursed her lips. "Will you hate me if I say that's begging for a 'famous last words' remark?"

Alexa laughed and tossed her napkin onto the table. "Not at all—I'm sure about this. Aside from the part where I think he's just a charming playboy who excels at manipulating people, I'm serious that I really don't believe in second runs. Over and over in my life, I've seen women take guys back after booting them out, and it always ends badly. There's a time in every relationship when the spark can take off and grow into something more, something special. If that chance is missed, it won't come back. All the things people do to recapture that moment just sours it 'til even the good times are remembered with pain. My heart is safer with Drew than any other man on this earth, 'cause he hasn't got any chance at all."

Keri watched Alexa for a minute then nodded. "Well, it's a good thing he's set up shop as our direct rival, then." She grinned and raised her coffee in a toast. "To enemies we love to hate."

Alexa laughed and raised her own cup to clink against Keri's. "To enemies."

Drew marked another nail sticking out at an odd angle with a bit of red tape then stepped back to scan the wall of what would be his office when the martial arts studio was finished.

Someone rapped on the doorframe behind him, and Drew looked up to see his buddy Aaron leaning there, the aerobic workout space behind him. Aaron was the manager of Handy Man Auto and Tire, so he was probably stopping by with news of Alexa's tire.

Drew excused himself from the electrician, who was doing a bit of post-drywall work on a problem outlet, and went to meet his friend. Alexa had been cluttering his thoughts since he'd left Crouching Tiger. He would be grateful to clear up the issue with her tire so he could put her out of his mind.

Aaron looked around with admiration. "The place is looking good."

"Thanks," Drew said. "We need to hang the doors, and some of the rooms still need to be painted, but it's coming along." He walked slowly, leading Aaron out of the workout room and into the front desk area. His buddy's limp was extra-pronounced today, but Drew knew Aaron would never ask him to slow down.

Opening the sliding glass door on the big industrial fridge behind the desk, Drew motioned to the energy drinks inside. "Want something?"

Aaron settled on a stool at the high counter. "Sure, I'll take one of those acai cocktails."

Drew passed the bottle over to Aaron then grabbed a GreenGo drink for himself and sat down across from his friend.

"So, how about that tire?" he asked.

Aaron took a sip of his drink. "The puncture is ragged, and wider on the inside. Too thin for a branch, and too high on the sidewall to be your typical road damage. There're no marks around it, so a scrape over the edge of a curb is unlikely."

Drew eyed his friend and swirled his drink. "You're saying it was slashed?"

"Most likely. Probably with a fair amount of force." Aaron took a long swallow then set the bottle down and faced Drew. "Of course, I can't be absolutely positive, but if it was my girl, I'd be all for setting up some good video surveillance and alerting the cops."

"That would be a smart move," Drew said.

Aaron grinned. "But it won't be happening?"

Drew shrugged. "Maybe. It's not my call right now. I was just collecting facts."

"Wow." Aaron gave a low whistle. "How did this person get you to do her toting and fact-finding but manage to cut you out of the decisions? The Drew I know doesn't get involved with a sticky situation unless he's in charge. It isn't family, is it?"

Drew shook his head and stood. Then he smiled and held out his hand for Aaron to shake. "Thanks for looking into this for me."

Aaron gripped his hand. "You're not going to tell me whose tire that was, are you?"

"Not just yet," Drew said. "It's not for me to say."

"Whatever." Aaron grinned, not seeming the least bit put out by Drew's discretion. He rose and limped toward the front door. "You know where to find me if your pretty bird needs a new tire to replace the one you brought in." He paused in the doorway and looked back at Drew. "Just keep an eye out for her, Drew. This guy wasn't fooling around."

Drew nodded and watched Aaron go. He gathered up their empty bottles and tossed them in the recycle bin. Was it possible Aaron had guessed whose tire he'd brought in? It was a small town, and there weren't many people Drew was likely to be toting tires for. Of course, Aaron had the advantage of knowing how besotted Drew had been with Alexa back in the day. He and Aaron had kept in touch after Drew graduated from Ranger school, so all through Drew's leave, Aaron had heard plenty about Drew's golden girl. Of course, he also knew that Alexa living in Willowdale was one reason Drew had been reluctant to make the town his home base at first.

In the end, the pull of the beautiful Willowdale property Drew had inherited from his grandfather had been enough to bring him back. Since Aaron had come to town—accepting the position at Handy Tire and Auto from a sympathetic veteran—he'd heard plenty of grumbling from Drew about how impossible Alexa was.

Yeah, Aaron had probably guessed it was Alexa's tire. But Drew trusted his friend to be discreet. He trusted his assessment of the tire, too, which didn't bode well for Alexa.

Drew walked back into the main workout room to see if the electrician had finished up. Maybe after he wrapped things up at the studio, he could stop by Alexa's place on his way home, tell her about her tire, and make sure she was set for the night. He knew it was none of his business and that she wouldn't thank him for his help. But he couldn't shake the feeling that she shouldn't be left to face this situation alone.

CHAPTER FOUR

A LEXA PULLED INTO HER DRIVEWAY and turned the car off. She opened the door and eased her foot out but hesitated to put weight on it. She'd forgotten to pack a spare pair of shoes that morning, so when she went home, she had to wear the black leather boots that went with her skirt. Normally, that wouldn't have been any big deal. But today, her bruised foot was feeling pinched in her boot, and it had been fussing at her all the way home.

Well, no reason to put up with it any longer. Alexa eased her boot off then gave her foot a minute to calm down before slipping off the other boot and climbing out of the car. The foot started to feel better the minute the pressure was off. It really wasn't that bad of a scrape; it just didn't like confinement.

She stretched it gently for a minute, letting herself enjoy the quiet of the night. Standing tall above her, the pines that took up most of her front yard seemed to whisper in the wind. The scent of cedar wafted down from her neighbor's tree, and all around her were the cute Cape Cods that lined her street. They weren't big houses. Only half of them had a garage, and hers wasn't one of those. Still, she loved the way the big trees gave the neighborhood a sheltered feel.

She put her feet out on the ground, and both protested the chill of the driveway. Either that, or her entire body was conspiring to punish her for that idiotic moment of distraction when she'd seen Drew. What had she been thinking?

It was time she put him out of her mind, and the easiest way to do that would be to get on with her work for the evening. Alexa grabbed her purse and the small box of books she needed to look over before the next morning then propped herself up against the car while she fished for her keys. *Oh yeah, my boots!* She slung her purse higher on her shoulder, piled the boots on the box, and dangled the keys from her pinkie finger. Good thing it wasn't far to her door.

She was just starting for the house when a truck pulled up and parked at her curb. Drew got out and shut the door.

It was the same thing all over again. She felt the same flash of pleasure at the sight of him, followed by the sick feeling of embarrassment and dread, not to mention anger that he could still affect her like that. Mother of Pearl, how could he still get under her skin?

Alexa turned her back on him and marched up to her door. At least, she tried to march. With her arms loaded and her bare feet flinching at the cold, it was more of a fast shuffle. She prayed it didn't look as though she was running scared. She offered the fates anything they wanted— even her secret stash of fuzzy cat sweaters she liked to pull out each Christmas—if only she could make it to her door and get safely inside before he caught up to her.

Apparently, the fates weren't interested. In a few long strides, Drew had cut across the lawn and stopped at the bottom of the steps. "Hey." He balanced on his toes, as if he was torn between coming and going. "I heard back on your tire and thought I'd stop by. Need a hand?"

Alexa fumbled with her keys, trying unsuccessfully to look poised and collected as she balanced her purse, the box of books, and her boots, all while standing in her bare feet.

Hopeless. Why exactly did she care if she looked poised in front of Drew, anyway? "So, what did they find? Can it be fixed?"

Drew shifted from one foot to the other. "There's a cut in the tire wall, so you'll need a new tire. It can't be patched, and it looks like it's—"

When Alexa realized where he was going, the keys slipped from her fingers and jangled onto the porch steps.

Drew reached down and picked them up. He flipped them once in his hand then met Alexa's eyes. "Your tire's been slashed. Do you know anyone who would do that? Anyone who might be angry or holding a grudge?"

"Besides you?" Alexa smiled sweetly at the astonishment on his face then turned her back on him. Okay, so maybe that was uncalled for. Between the stalker, slashed tire, and Drew showing up, acting as if he had a place in her life, she wasn't sure which way was up or down anymore.

She did know that she needed to dump her armful of books before she dropped them all at Drew's feet. Alexa steadied the box on the porch railing, hoping it would balance there. That was when she noticed a flash of movement. Something in the living room window caught her eye.

Ragbag, her kitten, stood on the ledge inside the window. He was soaking wet and dripping.

He meowed through the window then bent his head to lick his wet fur. His balance was off, and he wobbled before tumbling off the ledge.

"Ragbag!" Alexa snatched the keys from Drew's hand and unlocked the door in record time.

Dumping the big box on the couch, she bent beside Ragbag and examined him carefully. He was even soggier than he'd looked in the window, but he appeared okay aside from that. He jumped into her lap and purred ecstatically because she was home.

"Silly kitten, how'd you get wet?" Alexa asked. "The water dish?" Ragbag had been known to play in the water, but he'd never soaked himself.

Drew had followed her and stood in the doorway with his head cocked. "Is that running water I hear?"

"Running water?" Alexa caught the sound and got up, running as fast as she could manage down the hall to the bathroom. When she tried to open the door, she slammed into it. It was locked.

Through the door, she could hear water running and a weak meow.

Reaching up over her head, she ran her fingers along the top of the doorframe. Once upon a time, she had kept a small pick there, intended to open this kind of lock, but her searching fingers came up empty.

She slammed her fist into the closed door. "Damn!"

"Let me." Drew flipped open a micro tool and reached past her to fiddle with the lock. After a moment, the lock made an audible click, then the door swung open.

Alexa rushed in. Her two adult cats were in the bathtub, trapped underneath a laundry basket that had been flipped over to make a cage. The tap was turned on, and the water level in the tub had risen to the point that the cats were just barely keeping their heads above water. Even as she watched, Fieldgar's head slipped beneath the surface.

Snatching the basket out of the tub, Alexa tossed it aside and pulled Fieldgar free. She passed him to Drew, who crouched beside her, ready with a towel. Then she reached back for Oreo. When her black-and-white kitty was bundled in a towel, she looked around for Ragbag, who had followed them in, but Drew had already wrapped him in another towel.

"I... I don't..." Alexa stuttered to a stop. She put her face down close to Oreo's face and worked to calm her racing heart enough so she could get words out. Falling apart wouldn't help her cats—figuring this out would. She drew on the calm she reached for when sparring and lifted her head. "How did they get in the tub? And why was the water running?" She knew Drew didn't have the answers, but she needed him to get her thinking and help her sort out what had happened.

Instead of answering, he picked Fieldgar up and rubbed him vigorously then held him out to Alexa. "He's so limp, almost like he's asleep. Is that normal?"

She took Fieldgar and cradled him in her lap. She stroked his tiger-orange face then tickled him under the chin but got no response. "The water was cool, and cats hate water. Maybe he's in shock?"

"Maybe," Drew answered grimly. "But I wonder if that's all." He stood and started searching around the edge of the tub. After a minute, he held up a squeezable tube for Alexa to examine. "What's this?"

Alexa gasped. "Their sedative! I use it when they travel." She grabbed the tube then looked at her sleepy cats. Fieldgar was just this side of conscious, and Oreo wasn't much better. "I don't know how much they were given or how long they were in the water. I have to get them to the vet!"

"Right." Drew grabbed another towel from the stack on the shelf and rubbed down the empty laundry basket. Then he flipped it over and made a nest in the bottom for the cats. "You hold them; I'll drive."

"Right," Alexa answered. "Go start your truck."

In two minutes, they were speeding toward the animal hospital at the edge of town. Alexa knew the vet—his wife liked to come into Crouching Tiger for the early-morning cardio routine. Plus, the vet had taken care of her cats since she moved to Willowdale. She called the clinic's emergency number on the way, and he agreed to meet them there.

Ragbag poked his head out of the basket and meowed piteously.

"It's okay, baby," Alexa told him, stroking his fur. She spoke to Drew, needing interaction so she could keep herself together. "He hates car rides."

Drew glanced over at the cat. "I don't blame him. Everything about riding in a car must be disorienting for a cat."

Alexa nodded and settled Ragbag back into the nest of towels. Fieldgar's orange tiger stripes contrasted with Oreo's black-and-white fur. Ragbag sprawled across them both, adding his splotches of brown, orange, and black. Cuddled down in the towels, they looked almost like someone's idea of a laundry joke.

Alexa felt tears prick the back of her eyes. She blinked hard and fixed her eyes on the road. *They will be okay. They have to be.*

Drew glanced at her, and his hand moved as if to touch her. He pulled back, keeping both hands on the steering wheel. When he spoke, his tone was gentle to distract her and provide comfort. "When I was a kid, I used to love the big old tom that lived on my grandparents' farm—my mom's parents—in Pennsylvania. He was mean to most people, but he liked me. Probably because I used to share my ice cream with him."

Alexa smiled. "He ate from your bowl?"

"Worse." Drew shook his head ruefully. "I used to share my cone with him. We'd take turns, lick for lick, from each side."

The image surprised a laugh out of Alexa—a small one, but an improvement on the tears she'd felt a minute ago. The tightness in her chest eased, and her heart slowed to something closer to normal.

They pulled up to the clinic. Dr. Springer was waiting by the door, the light from the room behind him silhouetting his long shape. He led them to an examination table and took the cats out one by one.

Alexa caught herself holding her breath. The cats looked so floppy and shapeless that breathing seemed like a luxury she couldn't afford.

Dr. Springer unhooked the stethoscope from his ears after listening to Fieldgar's lungs and began moving his hands over the cat's body. "Do you have any idea how long they were in the tub?"

Alexa had filled him in over the phone on how she'd found the cats. Now, she scrunched her face, trying to think. "My house is on the older side, and the tub fills up slowly. So, maybe ten minutes? Or possibly fifteen?"

Drew shifted beside her. "The water wasn't warm like a bath would be, and cold-water pressure is usually faster than hot. I'd guess more like five to ten minutes."

Dr. Springer nodded and hooked the stethoscope in his ears so he could listen to Ragbag and Oreo. When it came time to take a small blood sample from each cat, Drew held Fieldgar, Alexa hung on to Oreo, and Dr. Springer took Ragbag. The cats were almost too cooperative, their sleepy state making them easy to examine.

A few minutes later, Dr. Springer set Oreo back in the basket beside Fieldgar and Ragbag then faced Alexa. "I won't know how much of the sedative they were given until I run the blood test, but I think they're going to be okay. Let me keep them here tonight, monitor their breathing, and make sure they stay warm and dry. Their lungs sound clear, so I don't think we have to worry about water inside."

Alexa nodded, smiling weakly. The relief that washed over her was so intense, she felt light-headed. "That sounds great. And thank you again, Dr. Springer. I really appreciate it."

"I'm happy to help," Dr. Springer said with a smile.

"Thank you," Alexa said. "I'll call in the morning."

She followed Drew out to the truck and slumped against the seat. Of course now that her adrenaline was wearing off, her foot was smarting again, and she felt as though she would rather be almost anywhere else. She kept herself well over to her side of the truck so there was no chance of physical contact with Drew. It wasn't so much that she didn't trust him as she didn't trust herself. In her weakened state, it was harder to be sure of her emotions. She was suddenly intensely aware of his warm, solid body and the way he'd worked in sync with her to take care of her babies.

Drew shut his door and started the truck. Then he glanced over at her and spoke gently. "You need to call the police. They'll want to dust your house for fingerprints."

Alarm shot through Alexa, and her breathing sped up. Someone had been in her house—someone with a really nasty way of showing his affection. The cats should be safe at the clinic, but her problems were just beginning. Drew was absolutely right. It was time to call the police.

She fumbled in her purse and pulled her cell out, but she didn't dial 9-1-1 or the police station. She knew someone on the force—Detective Rawlings. The detective was a mom who had twin boys in the school's Little Tiger program, and she often came in to watch her boys' classes when she was off duty. If Alexa had to call in the police, she was at least getting the help of someone she knew.

Detective Rawlings picked up on the second ring. Their conversation was short and to the point. When Drew pulled up in front of Alexa's house, there was already a black-and-white police car parked in front. Detective Rawlings was getting out of a second, unmarked car.

The detective met them on the lawn. "Wait here while the uniforms check for an intruder." Her voice was cool and professional, but she gave Alexa a little squeeze on the arm before directing two uniformed officers to check the house over. She sent a third to walk around to the back. When the officers gave them the all clear, she led Alexa and Drew into the living room.

Detective Rawlings settled into a chair by the coffee table and pulled out a notebook. Her blond hair was smoothed back in a business-like cut, and her clear blue eyes seemed to catch every detail. Her air of competence gave Alexa the sense that everything was under control. "Start at the beginning and tell me everything you can remember," she told Alexa.

Drew leaned against the bookcase, and Alexa sat on the couch, facing Detective Rawlings. She took a deep breath and told her about the unexplained gifts and notes.

"It started a few weeks ago when someone left a pretty pumpkin-orange candle in my office at Crouching Tiger. My name was written on the bottom in gold glitter, and the way it sat on the edge of my desk made me think a child had stepped in and put it there."

Detective Rawlings looked up from her notes. "The office door wasn't locked? Was it closed?"

Alexa shook her head. "It's open during the afternoon when we have classes going on. Parents can leave a check on the desk or a note for one of us to call them. Kids don't usually wander in, but it has happened."

Detective Rawlings nodded and made a note.

Alexa continued. "Then a week later, a box of snickerdoodles—my favorite cookie—was left in the book deposit box at the library. It was wrapped in my favorite comic strip and had my name written on it." She bit her lip, anticipating the next question. "Unfortunately, I threw the paper away after opening it. I thought it was left by one of the kids from our story hour, who'd baked some treats and wanted to share. I didn't think about it maybe being creepy until later."

Detective Rawlings nodded, her face showing no judgment. Drew shifted from his place in front of the bookcase, but Alexa didn't let herself look at him.

"Then finally, a card was left in the office at the school, congratulating me on my win in an intraschool tournament. It wasn't signed, but it had a typed note, and my name looked the same as it did on the comic strip that was wrapped around the cookies. Hand-printed letters—kind of blocky." Alexa blew out a breath. "That was the first I realized something was off, because the card was a little creepy, and the note was worse. It talked about things I'd been doing, things no one knew but me. And it was creepy in its praise. That was when I realized I had a stalker."

"Do you have it here?" Detective Rawlings asked.

Alexa nodded and rose. After a few seconds of rummaging through her papers, she handed over the hated card and note, plus their envelope.

The detective studied them a moment then handed them to a uniformed officer. "And the candle? Is it here?"

"No, it's still at Crouching Tiger. On the desk in the office." Alexa paused then gave a little shrug. "That's it, except for the slash to my tire and the attack on my cats today."

"You mentioned your tire being slashed," Detective Rawlings said. "Let's go over the details now."

Alexa nodded and tried to give a cold and factual account of finding her tire slashed and Drew's help. This was the opposite of the dramatized story she'd given Keri earlier. With the detective asking questions at appropriate moments, Alexa filled her in on what had happened that evening after she had seen Ragbag in the window.

When Alexa stopped, the detective waited with her pen poised. "Is there anything else? Anyone you can think of who would top a list of suspects?"

Alexa shook her head. Willowdale was a friendly town, and she'd believed she was on good terms with pretty much everyone—except possibly Drew, but even he had been nothing but a help with her cats.

"It may be someone from your past," Detective Rawlings said gently. "Old enemies can come back to haunt in situations like these. Have you had any contact with Jason Stone since the trial?"

"You know about that?" Alexa asked, startled. Even hearing Jason's name made her shiver, and she felt herself curling inward.

"Who is Jason Stone?" Drew asked sharply. "What trial?"

Detective Rawlings glanced at him then at Alexa and said nothing. She clearly understood that it wasn't her story to tell.

Alexa rubbed her hands over her face then folded them in her lap and spoke as evenly as she could. "A little over three years ago, just before I started on my master's, a boy came into the campus bookstore where I worked and attacked one of my coworkers, Sierra. They had been in a hot-and-cold relationship for a while, but Sierra had finally broken it off for good, and I guess he decided to kill her. Thankfully, he didn't succeed. When his case went to trial, I testified against him. His sentence was five to ten years, so he should still be in jail."

"The part she left out is that she saved her coworker's life," Detective Rawlings said dryly. "Jason Stone fought with his ex-girlfriend and stabbed her. Then he went for her throat and would have killed her if Alexa hadn't stopped him."

Alexa said nothing, her eyes on her hands. She hadn't felt like a hero, just terribly frightened. She also felt incredibly guilty that she hadn't moved faster and prevented her friend from receiving the long scar that ran from her neck down her chest. For months afterward, Alexa had been afraid to be alone, panicked whenever someone moved suddenly. It was one reason she'd taken up martial arts again—to give her some feeling of control in her life.

Detective Rawlings broke the silence. "It will be easy enough to find out if Mr. Stone has been paroled or is still in jail. Let's hope he's still locked up." She turned to Drew. "You were there for the tire change and helped again tonight. Tell me what you remember."

As Drew gave details about the tire and answered the detective's questions, Alexa listened carefully. She was no expert in these matters, but it sounded as if the detective was probing Drew to see if he could be the stalker, and for the first time, Alexa considered that thought. After all the things she'd said about him, he certainly had reason to dislike her. And he'd been close at hand after the two previous attacks, so it was possible he could have arranged them in order to play the part of the gallant knight and save her.

But even before hearing his alibis—complete with people who could vouch for his whereabouts when the attacks had taken place—she knew Drew hadn't done it. She may have found him the most aggravating person in the world, but she also knew he wasn't the kind of man who would frighten or stalk a woman. Whatever his faults were in the romance arena and however much he might have bruised her heart, he wasn't creepy like that. She could sense in her core that she was safe with him in the room. It was a wonderful feeling—one she knew could become addictive if given the chance.

When Drew finished retelling the events of the day, Detective Rawlings flipped her notebook to a new page. "There's no sign of forced entry," she told Alexa. "You're sure it was locked?"

She nodded.

"Does anyone else have a key? Or know the location of your spare? Is there anyone who has regular access to your keys and could have made a copy?"

Alexa had started to shake her head, but she froze at that last question and made a rueful sound. "When I'm acting as head instructor in the dojo, my keys hang on a hook just inside the office door. Anyone who needs to get into the storage closet can grab them then put them back. You don't think...?"

Detective Rawlings nodded. "You're right. I've seen students and instructors grab the set hanging there, though I didn't know they were yours. Someone could have made a wax copy to be made permanent later or just borrowed your house key off the loop for an hour or two then put it back. It could even have been someone off the street who knows your habits." She exchanged a grim look with Drew. "We have to assume that they have a complete set and can come and go from your home as they please. At least until you can get the locks changed."

Alexa's blood suddenly chilled, and she was uncomfortably aware of how exposed she was, sitting with her back to the window. Her stalker could be watching her right now.

She shifted in her seat, resisting the urge to get up. Her hands balled into fists. Police were crawling all over the house, checking for fingerprints and looking for any evidence of the stalker. The haven she'd come home to every night since moving to Willowdale was no longer safe.

It was happening again. This was what she'd felt like after Jason Stone's attack—as if there was nowhere safe, and every situation could go from normal to terrifying and dangerous without warning. It was the worst feeling in the world.

Detective Rawlings leaned forward, and her voice took on a gentle tone. "Do you have someone you can stay with tonight? Someone you can trust, whose home is secure?"

Alexa shook her head, a sharp negative. "I won't put my friends in danger."

She rose and paced the length of her living room. It had suddenly gone from cozy to confining, as if she were trapped. "Besides, whoever made a copy of my keys knows me and could guess where I'd go. If they knew to take my keys, they could have taken the keys of any other black belt instructor—they're all my closest friends."

Drew spoke up from his stance against the bookcase. "You can stay with me."

45

CHAPTER FIVE

Alexa gave Drew a sharp look. "What?"

The way he stood, his broad shoulders tense beneath his shirt, his body ready for anything—it reminded her that he'd been a soldier. However, it was the warmth and fierce protection shining in his eyes that made her drop her gaze. "Thank you, but no. We're not even friends."

Detective Rawlings's eyes were speculative when she looked at Drew. "You realize that if something unexplained happens to her, you'll be our first suspect?" She held up a hand when he opened his mouth to answer. "Moreover, the escalation of the attacks indicates some shift in the stalker's psyche. Slashing Alexa's tire may have been done to isolate and scare her. When she accepted your help instead of being frightened— and received an offer of help from Stuart—the stalker stepped up the threat and attacked her in her home. If he were to find out she'd taken refuge with you… let's just say I wouldn't want to be in your shoes. You understand my meaning?"

Drew nodded, his jaw set in determined lines.

Detective Rawlings turned to Alexa. "I realize there's some rivalry between your schools, but you couldn't find a better bodyguard in Willowdale than Drew Cosimo. We've had him working with the police force on self-defense and de-escalation techniques, and he knows his stuff. The point that you're not friends would also work in your favor. The stalker is less likely to guess where you are."

"My granddad's house is sturdy and secure," Drew said, speaking almost as if he couldn't help himself. "It's down a private drive with a good view of anyone who might try to approach the house. I've added a safe room and replaced the old windows with shatter-proof glass." He lifted one shoulder in a shrug when Alexa looked at him in surprise. "I wanted to know how hard it would be to set it up properly, since home security is something people ask me about."

Alexa shifted where she stood. She had it on the tip of her tongue to refuse again, but her mind took that moment to replay the cries of her cats and the sound of running water behind a locked door. Underneath those sounds were the old images of a knife flashing down and a face contorted with rage. She walked to the window.

Night had fallen on her little neighborhood, but a warm light shone onto the street from the many windows in her neighbor's houses, and the old-fashioned streetlights added to the glowing look of a tiny Christmas village. It was really the perfect neighborhood for a single woman. It allowed her to be completely independent, yet she was still in the middle of a caring community. But as she stared out the window, the pools of shadows seemed to darken. The trees, which had felt so sheltering, now seemed to tower over the little homes.

She had worked so hard to gain back a feeling of security and sanity after the attack that day in the bookstore. Was she really going to run from her home and abandon everything she'd worked for? On the other hand, she knew her training was limited to hand-to-hand, which would do little good against someone who was armed with a gun. She also knew from her time sparring that it was tough for a woman to overpower a bigger, stronger man, and doubly so if he was psychotic and she had a normal aversion to causing someone harm.

What did Keri say? Something about not letting my fierce independence prevent me from accepting help when I need it.

She took a deep breath then faced Drew and Detective Rawlings. "I'll go pack a bag."

Drew watched Alexa as she left the room and hoped the surprise he felt didn't show on his face. He wasn't entirely sure what had prompted him to offer his place as her hideout, but he definitely hadn't expected her to take him up on it.

He wanted her somewhere safe, and he wasn't being arrogant in his belief that he could best provide that, but was this really a good idea? Alexa was a mess, and she hated him to the core. He couldn't entirely blame her. He hadn't treated her well at the end of his leave. He'd thought he was all that. He'd graduated Ranger school, for crying out loud, but he'd still been kind of a punk kid underneath the uniform.

And of course setting up shop in Willowdale as her rival hadn't helped their relationship. He wouldn't tell Alexa, but her little digs had found every sore spot that remained from his youth as an army brat. Every army kid dealt with some flak from civilians, and in his case, there was plenty of that to go around since he'd been raised by a single father, who didn't have time to teach his son smoother manners.

Alexa's contempt had rubbed salt into old wounds he had thought were healed. He rolled his shoulders to ease the tension growing there. He would treat protecting her like a mission. She was just another hostage he had to keep alive and safe until the job was done and she was out of his hair.

"So, a safe room, huh?" Something in Detective Rawlings's voice snagged Drew's attention.

"That's right." He couldn't read the detective's expression. Was she laughing at him? "Nothing fancy, not like the movies. Just a room that's been reinforced where possible. I installed a sturdy frame and a solid, reinforced door. Then added two deadbolts that slide straight into solid wood."

Detective Rawlings nodded. There was definitely a glint in her eye, and a smile played about her lips. "And that room would be... where? Not the kitchen or living room?"

"My bedroom, actually." Drew caught the suggestion in her look and shook his head emphatically. "Only to be used in emergencies. Besides, the guest bedroom is also a safe room." He didn't add that he only considered the guest room a backup, considering it was on the main floor and had a window with easy access to the ground.

The detective grinned. "I only ask because I don't want to save Alexa from the stalker only to charge her with assault and battery. She doesn't like you very much."

Drew winced. "I'm aware of that. But I know how to keep my cool and neutralize a situation. I'll keep things on the level and keep Alexa at arm's length."

The detective nodded again then flipped her notebook shut and stood. Her face turned serious. "I wouldn't have pushed her to stay with you, but my gut doesn't like what I'm getting here. The bathroom door was shut and locked when the two of you tried to get in, but the one kitten was out and free." Her voice had a careful note, indicating she was sharing a guess. "I suspect the stalker had only just exited the house when you arrived. The water hadn't had time to swamp the tub, and he might have been looking for the escaped kitten. If Alexa hadn't stopped on the doorstep and talked to you, it's even possible she would have walked in on him."

Drew felt as if someone had kicked him in the stomach. His mind began supplying scenarios in which the stalker attacked Alexa as she walked through the door or waited to surprise her when she headed for the shower. With each ugly scenario, his protective instincts went up a notch, and he had to remind himself that nothing had happened. Alexa was safe, and she would stay that way.

He took a deep breath and let it out slowly. "Do you think Alexa realizes?"

Detective Rawlings shook her head. "I doubt it. At this point, she's just coping with the obvious and trying to absorb her new reality. Try to get her to eat tonight. And make sure there're plenty of blankets in that guest bedroom in case she feels chilled in the aftermath of what's happened to her cats, not to mention the emotional shock of having been forced from her home."

Drew nodded. Thankfully, he kept a well-stocked fridge and knew how to cook. He'd learned during the year he spent taking care of his dad, after his dad's cancer was diagnosed as terminal. Offering food that was one hundred percent homemade had been the only way he could coax his picky and ailing father to eat.

"Do you carry?"

The detective's question brought Drew back to the present. Of course she would want to know if he kept a gun on him. He nodded. "I'm not carrying today, but I always keep my permit on me." He pulled it from his wallet and held it out. "I have a couple concealed holsters I'm comfortable using."

The detective looked over his concealed carry license then handed it back to him. "I thought you might. Glad to see you keep your permit on you."

She looked as if she might say more, but just then, Alexa came back downstairs with a garment bag slung over her shoulder and a duffel in her hand. Her limp had disappeared during the push of the evening, but now it was back and possibly more pronounced. He was sure her body was feeling the effects of the emotional ringer she'd been put through.

Drew took the bags from her then walked out and put them in the truck. When he came back for Alexa, she and Detective Rawlings were making a list of black belts at the school who were also instructors. It sounded as though the detective planned to keep an eye on them for any strange behavior. She also planned to watch their homes in case the stalker had made a copy of their keys as well.

Detective Rawlings followed Drew and Alexa out to the truck.

"This is the real deal, guys." Her face was serious, and she spoke in that official officer voice that Drew knew well. "We don't know what this guy is capable of. Call if you see anything suspicious or remember something that might be helpful. Any leads at all will help us narrow down the list of possible suspects."

Drew nodded, but he was only giving the detective half his attention. Alexa's house and yard were crawling with cops, but that didn't mean the stalker wasn't watching. He could be hiding in the bushes. He could even be one of Alexa's neighbors. They needed to get Alexa out of there.

Detective Rawlings put out her hand to touch Alexa's shoulder. "I'll need to meet with you and get a list of men you've dated in the last year or two, plus anyone who may hold a grudge or feel they have a score to settle. You'll be at the dojo tomorrow for sparring?"

Alexa nodded. "With my foot banged up, I'll just be watching, but they're counting on me to unlock in the morning. Besides," she said around a feeble grin, "surely I'll be safe in the middle of a dozen loyal black belts."

Drew squinted at an open garage a few houses down and across the street. Was there someone in there? If someone standing there had binoculars, he could watch their every move and easily identify Drew's truck. He could then follow them to Drew's house.

"I'll come by and talk with you then," Detective Rawlings said. "And pick up the gift candle you mentioned. I'll also need to take your fingerprints so we can rule them out."

Alexa nodded.

"That'll be fine," Drew said. "Thank you for your help." He opened the truck's passenger door for Alexa then gave Detective Rawlings a quick nod before climbing into the driver's seat. It was time to get Alexa home.

CHAPTER SIX

A LEXA WAS QUITE SURE HER body had a mean sense of humor. Why else—after the day she'd had—would she find herself much too aware of Drew's masculine form beside her and the toned guns of his biceps? She felt a flare of heat spark between them when he reached toward her to shift gears. She had known Drew, the young man. What would the mature stud be like?

Shaking her head for actually entertaining that thought, even silently, Alexa looked away from Drew and focused on the scenery out the window. Comfortable definitely wasn't the word she was looking for, but something felt *right* about sitting beside Drew and relying on him for the physical protection she needed at the moment. Something about it clicked. Although that surprised Alexa, it was nothing compared with the shock of Drew offering his place at all. True, people acted differently when there was a crisis, and an aggressive stalker certainly counted as an emergency. So, did two shockers make a normal?

Of course, what was "normal" between Drew and her had included a great deal of physical touching and intimacy. She would have to be smoking something to indulge in that now. What was it her aunt used to say? Every good chemist knew when to keep it contained. That was just how Alexa planned to manage this situation—containment, with nothing more than cool professionalism between them.

They turned onto the long, winding road that led to Drew's house, and Alexa rounded up her wandering thoughts. The house came into view, and Alexa caught her breath. She didn't remember it having such charm. When Drew's grandfather had lived here, he'd been the dean of the college, and she'd been a little intimidated by him.

Now she could appreciate the house as a lovely colonial revival tucked into the trees. The home was complete with a charming gabled roof and crisp white accents around the windows that contrasted with the deep red of the brick. In addition to the traditional square colonial box, the house had a wing off each side on the ground floor. Warm lights shone brightly from the windows, and a lamp stood in a little garden to the right side of the front door. Completing the picture was a bench in the garden, waiting for someone to come and sit. Appearing as it did around a bend in the road, the house made Alexa feel as though she were coming home to the family hearth she'd never known.

"You like it?" Drew's tone was studiously casual.

Alexa nodded. "I don't remember it having such homey warmth or such character."

"I added the gardens. Maybe that's what you're noticing." Drew pulled into the detached garage and parked the truck. "I want the house to be a good place for a family to live."

Alexa nodded, not sure what to say to that. Didn't having a family involve commitment and settling down, preferably with one woman? How exactly did he plan to manage that? He'd spent all his growing-up years popping around the country. Surely his time as a Ranger hadn't been any more settled.

Drew grabbed her garment and duffel bags and got out of the truck. Alexa limped after him. They went through the back door into the kitchen, and Alexa paused to smile as she took it in. This space had also been updated and seemed like a perfect haven.

The granite counters were a creamy white with red sandstone streaks, and the cabinets were a warm wood. Low-hanging lights shed a bright glow onto the long island in the center of the kitchen, and stainless-steel pots and pans hung on the underside of a pantry shelf. Everything was in reach of the stove and sink, ready for the chef.

"Don't tell me you've learned to cook and can make use of this kitchen," Alexa said with a teasing grin.

Drew arched his eyebrows and gave her a look of mock ferocity.

"Disparage my cooking skills at your own risk. My culinary arts can make you abandon all common sense and embrace never-before-considered indulgent delicacies."

Alexa laughed, the sound coming out a little more breathless than she had intended. Looking at that warm, intense look in Drew's eyes, she could almost forget the jagged wedge of hurt and animosity between them. Almost. She made her smile merely polite. "I look forward to a demonstration."

Drew nodded. "Consider it done." He waved her through the kitchen and led her down a short hall with a bathroom door and a row of closets. Alexa followed him, though it had just occurred to her that he was leading her to her bedroom… and once again, her imagination took off in all kinds of wild fantasies. First among them was the image of Drew stopping—anywhere in the hallway would be fine—and turning to her. He would swear his undying love for her and confess that he'd been taken over by an alien or acting on secret operative orders when he'd been so rude to her. They would stare into each other's eyes, mouths parting, and time would slow down. Then they would rush into a tender embrace and tear each other's clothes off. That was where her conscious mind pulled up.

They would rush into a tender embrace and tear each other's clothes off? Like either of them would be stupid enough to pull a stunt like that with a stalker on the loose. Moreover, she didn't even like Drew, and she wasn't the kind of girl to jump into bed with a guy she didn't like. She shook her head, hard, and was grateful for the dark hallway, which hid the heat she could feel in her face. By the time they reached the guest bedroom at the end of the hall, Alexa thought she had her libido under control. All the same, she decided to pass on going in the bedroom with Drew—not when just being in his house made her insides all warm and melted, like gooey chocolate chip cookies straight out of the oven.

She waited outside the bedroom door while Drew went in and hung her garment bag in the closet. When he came out, she moved to go inside and quickly realized her mistake. By staying out in the hall, she'd left them hardly any room to pass each other. Would Drew think she'd done it on purpose? That she'd accepted his invitation for safety with the intent of getting in his bed?

Her already-warm face flamed, and she tried to keep as much space as possible between them as she passed.

Unfortunately, that backfired. She bumped into the doorjamb and bounced off it.

"Easy." Drew's strong arms came up to steady Alexa, partially circling her. He smelled of cedar, sunshine, and something else, something that was just Drew. He flashed a grin, his white teeth a stark contrast to his tanned skin and black hair. His touch simultaneously took her breath away and embarrassed her with its intimacy, raising goose bumps along her arms. What was with her tonight? She usually had better self-control. It must be some kind of post-traumatic turn-on.

"Sorry." She jerked free and stepped inside the bedroom, shutting the door before her flaming red face could give her away.

She leaned against the door and listened to the sound of Drew's footsteps moving down the hall. What had she been thinking, coming here?

Simple, that she had a stalker and nowhere else to go.

Alexa took a deep, steadying breath and told herself to get a grip. She hadn't thrown herself at Drew, nor was she a besotted and desperate ex-girlfriend trying to rekindle the flame. She was a professional, intelligent enough to know when she needed help facing down a problem. Drew was giving her that help, but his doing so changed nothing between them.

Time to get her mind on other things. Alexa pushed away from the door and took a look around the guest bedroom. Most of the furniture was a gorgeous aged mahogany and looked sturdy in the way handcrafted items did. The warm tones of the furniture were accented with a vase of white asters that looked almost real on a side table, and delicate white curtains at the window. Framed photos hung on the walls, showing everyday scenes in European towns.

Alexa moved closer to one photo showing a flower market on a bridge in Italy. She noticed the small signature in the bottom right-hand corner. "Dan Cosimo." Drew's father.

Walking around the room, she studied each picture. A church

in the background of one photo identified the picture as taken in Wales. In the foreground was an old lady showing her knitting to her freckled granddaughter.

Alexa was pretty sure she was looking at the canals of St. Petersburg in another picture, but the foreground showed a young man with black hair, painting on his easel. A second picture taken in Russia revealed snow piled high over village roofs. A crisp sun rose behind them, and shades of pink lit the onion domes in the distance.

The last photo was a close-up of an older building. Vines climbed the walls, and a lovely wooden door was set back in a deep encasement. A black knocker in the center of the door and the stylistic carving of a lionlike face at the top of the casement added a fascinating touch to an otherwise common scene. If she had to hazard a guess, Alexa would place that door as German, but she couldn't be sure, just as she was only guessing that the close-up of tulips was taken in Holland.

Alexa sat on the bed and looked around. She'd never been to Europe or anywhere else so exotic, but looking at these pictures, she almost felt as if she had. The photographs had a clarity to them, and the mature composition rivaled anything she'd seen published in the travel magazines she loved to pore over in the library. How had Drew's father learned to take pictures like that, and why hadn't he become a professional photographer?

She didn't remember much about Dan Cosimo. She'd only met him once, briefly, when he had come to see Drew for an afternoon while Drew was staying with his granddad. She understood Dan Cosimo was military of some kind, like Drew, but she didn't know which branch. Who would've guessed that the tall, rigid man she'd met had such an eye for capturing the soul of a place in film? It made her wonder how well she knew any of the people she saw every day. After all, if the stalker wasn't Jason Stone, he was most likely hiding among her acquaintances.

Alexa's cell phone rang, making her jump just a little.

The number was Keri's. "Hello?"

"Hey, how's the foot? Is it going to keep you from opening for sparring tomorrow?" Keri asked.

"No, it's sore but not bad. I'm still planning on coming." Alexa tucked the phone against her shoulder and started unpacking the garment bag.

"Great, 'cause after sparring, a bunch of us are going to the Saturday street festival. Want to come? We can grab seats by the bands so we're not walking much."

Normally, the Saturday street festival was a favorite pastime of Alexa's, but the crowds and commotion sounded like a recipe for disaster right now. The festival would be the ideal environment for her stalker, because she wouldn't know him from the rest of the crowd. Alexa had to suppress a shudder. "Talk about creepy," she muttered.

"What's that?" Keri asked, surprised.

"Oh, nothing," Alexa said. "Just that I think I'll pass on the festival tomorrow." She wanted to tell her friend what was going on, but Detective Rawlings had told her not to tell anyone where she was staying, and that included even Keri.

Alexa went on. "I doubt my foot will be up for it after sparring, so I'll probably go into the library and catch up on cataloging and sorting the latest donations. With the big sale on Tuesday, I shouldn't fall behind."

"How much is your foot hurting?" Keri sounded concerned. "Do you need me to come over and help you carry books or whatever in the morning?"

"No, I'll be fine." Alexa stretched her foot out to look at. She didn't want Keri to stop by her house the next morning and find her missing. "It's a bit puffy, but the bruising and scrapes are all surface. I'm using it mostly normally now... but I do need to get those library books done."

"It's probably smarter if you take it easy tomorrow, anyway." Even though Keri agreed, she sounded a little bummed. "I'm glad your reason for skipping the festival is just your foot. You had me worried for a minute there that this stalker got to you somehow and warned you away from your friends."

Alexa winced but forced a laugh. "If he tries that, I'll be sure to warn him about a black belt's loyalty."

"Sounds like a plan." Keri's voice sounded distant for a second, as if she'd looked away. "I better go. See you tomorrow."

Alexa hung up then sat back down on the bed and looked at her phone. It was hard, keeping things from her friend. And she didn't think it would really have hurt anyone to tell Keri about the stalker's latest attack and what he'd done to her cats.

She got up and limped around, unpacking. The trouble was, Keri would want to hear all about it and demand to know where Alexa was staying and how she was safe. And in truth, Alexa couldn't be absolutely positive Keri would keep the secret that she was staying with Drew. Her friend would mean well, but Keri wasn't naturally suspicious, so she might spill something to someone she shouldn't because she didn't see them as a threat.

No, it was better for now if Alexa just stayed quietly hidden, with only her, Drew, and Detective Rawlings in on the game. While lying to her friend wasn't her favorite thing, it did have the plus side of postponing the embarrassing questions Keri was sure to ask about Drew.

As Alexa closed the closet door, a delicious smell wafted into the bedroom, and her stomach rumbled in response. It had been hours since she'd had a quick bite at Marcellino's, and she hadn't eaten a whole lot before that. Lucky for her, it smelled as though Drew was making good on his promise of food.

She grabbed her toiletry bag and stepped out into the hall, turning away from the kitchen and heading toward the bathroom she'd noticed at the end of the hall. If Drew was going to go all out and cook for her, the least she could do was look presentable when she showed up at the table. Not because she wanted to impress him, of course. She just didn't want to be the one shabby thing in his beautiful house.

Drew heard a door open and shut down the hall, and his gut tightened in anticipation of Alexa joining him. It was ridiculous, really. From the way his nerves were spiking, it felt as if he'd been called up before the colonel.

He added the asiago cheese to the salad and tossed it then set it on the table and stepped back. He didn't know how hungry she would be or what food she liked best, so he'd gone Mediterranean and whipped up several small dishes. Alexa could pick and choose what she wanted and hopefully find something that suited her.

She stopped in the kitchen doorway, and her eyes roamed hungrily over the dishes arranged on the table. When she looked at Drew, he put on his most charming smile and pulled out her chair.

She stepped forward. "Clearly, I was wrong to challenge you. This all smells amazing."

"An amazing meal for an amazing lady." When she stopped short, Drew realized instantly that she took his comment as a compliment of her looks—and didn't appreciate it. He plowed on. "What you did tonight, the way you handled yourself with your cats, you were amazing."

Alexa flushed a little, but she continued to her chair and sat. Drew caught a scent of something citrusy as he pushed in her chair. Her hair fell in smooth waves of honey brown and looked incredibly touchable. She'd freshened up before she came out, he was sure of it, and his chest swelled a little that she'd taken the trouble. Drew took his own seat across from Alexa.

She cleared her throat, but her voice still sounded a little husky when she spoke. Maybe she was as nervous as he was. "What do we have here? I recognize some of these but don't know their names."

She sounded impressed, and Drew felt a flood of pride. "The one with the shrimp is couscous paella, and beside it is roasted eggplant and feta, which you can dip with pita chips. This orange soup is a pumpkin curry soup, and then of course there's the salad, which has asiago cheese."

"Wow." Alexa's eyes spoke her enjoyment, and she made an appreciative sound after popping in a chip full of the eggplant and feta.

Drew couldn't help himself; he spooned up a bit of the pumpkin soup and passed it to her. "Here, try this."

She barely hesitated before taking the bait, and when she did, her eyes flew wide open and her mouth made a sensuous little pout. "Mmm, that's good!"

Drew grinned and just managed to stop himself from spoon-feeding it to her. He was getting way too much of a thrill out of feeding her. While he would like to think it was all motivated by a protective desire to follow Detective Rawlings's orders and make sure Alexa ate, the burning in his groin said otherwise. He could watch her eat all evening without caring about his own food, if only she'd let him.

Alexa took another bite, again with obvious enjoyment. *Down, boy!* He hadn't gotten where he was in life by following his baser instincts wherever they led him, and he wasn't about to start now. He hadn't even been thinking about the fact that Alexa still hated his guts and, moreover, had a stalker creep gunning for her. No way was he going to be the man she chose as her only alternative to a stalker.

Time for a little idle conversation to lighten things up. Too bad he sucked at chitchat. Drew cleared his throat. "It's a good thing I made it to the store yesterday and had the pumpkin and eggplant on hand. Otherwise, we would have had nothing but spaghetti."

"Spaghetti's good too," Alexa said.

She puckered her lips as she blew on her soup, and Drew's imagination instantly replaced the soup with her slurping on a long, skinny spaghetti noodle. He shifted in his seat.

"Where did you learn to cook like this?" Alexa asked.

Drew shrugged but mentally leapt at the chance to get his mind out of the gutter. "I spent time in the Mediterranean while on assignment, and I liked the food. While Dad was having chemo, he needed to eat, but he didn't have much of an appetite, so I taught myself to cook. Dad always loved homemade European food."

Alexa tilted her head, her eyes on his face. "Your dad spent a lot of time in Europe, I take it?"

Drew nodded. "We were based out of Europe for several years. Germany, Italy, Greece."

"Is that when he took the photos? I saw some from Russia too. And one in Wales." She added salad to her plate and dug in.

"You recognized the church in Wales?" Drew asked, impressed.

Alexa colored a bit. "I like to study history, and sometimes I look at travel magazines."

He opened his mouth to ask if she would ever like to visit Wales but caught himself just in time. What was he thinking? It would sound as though he were asking her to go with him, and no way was that a good idea.

He took a quick bite of soup to cover his pause. "I think he took those trips after I was grown, though it's hard to say." Drew kept his tone casual and watched Alexa take a bite of salad. "He was MI, so we never knew for sure where he was on assignment."

"MI–that's military intelligence, right?" Alexa asked. "Aren't those assignments pretty dangerous?"

Drew nodded. "Sometimes—though much of it is paperwork and analysis. But if he was doing any dangerous work in the field, he was always protected by Special Forces. That's part of why I became a Ranger. As a Ranger, I was a part of the military teams that used to keep my dad safe."

Alexa went still. "What a beautiful thought. Did your dad know that's how you saw it?"

Drew shrugged a little uncomfortably. "I don't know. Maybe. We swapped stories some, while I was taking care of him, but I don't know if it ever came up."

Nodding, Alexa took another bite, but Drew didn't try to fill the conversation lull.

How was it that he'd just told Alexa something so personal that he'd never even explained it to his dad? Was it just because she was female and easier to talk to? Or was it something more? And if there was something more, what did that mean for him?

CHAPTER SEVEN

DREW FELT AS IF A grenade had gone off inside his head. Of course he'd known he was attracted to Alexa. But there was a long way from attraction to suspecting he still had feelings for her. Trusting her, on a visceral level, made opening up to her feel perfectly natural. Why had it never occurred to him that he could want more from Alexa than a positive business relationship? Probably because he knew he would never have a chance with her.

But if someone had told him a week ago that tonight he would be watching her savor his couscous paella after dropping her overnight bag in his guest bedroom, he would have told them to get their head checked. Besides, once a Ranger, always a Ranger. And Rangers could do anything they set their minds to.

He smiled to himself at that thought. His gut reaction to anyone telling him he couldn't do something had always been to go out and do it. But no way was he really dumb enough to pursue Alexa just because she was hard to catch. His training—and his life since leaving his battalion—had taught him to consider his objective carefully and make sure the goal justified its pursuit.

And that left him right back where he started, with a gut saying go and a head holding back. He shook off the entire issue and set his mind to dealing with the mission at hand: keeping Alexa safe from her stalker.

To that end, he scooped a chunk of dip onto his pita and set about getting some intel. "You mentioned a sparring class. What time do you need to roll in the morning? And what time will you wrap up your day?"

"Saturday sparring is from nine to noon. We split the students into two groups, based on age, and give them each an hour and a half." Alexa set down her spoon, though her food was only half gone. "Afterwards, I'll need to meet with Detective Rawlings. I can do that somewhere handy to the dojo, so you won't need to pick me up 'til a little later. Maybe I can call when I'm ready?"

"Sure, whenever is good." Drew scraped up the last of his dip. "I've got some paperwork to go over, but I can do it while you're in class."

"Thanks, I really appreciate it. I won't have any trouble finding ways to keep busy at the dojo if you need more time." Alexa rose. She picked up her dishes and went to the sink to rinse them. When Drew brought his to the sink, she rinsed them, too, and started the dishwasher.

Drew smiled as he popped lids on the leftovers and put them in the fridge. The scene was so peaceful and domestic, something he had no experience with, at least not with a woman as part of it.

Alexa took a last swipe at the kitchen table then rinsed the cloth and hung it out. "Thanks for the dinner. It was delicious." She smiled at him, warm and... surely, that was an admiring look. But when he returned the smile and shifted toward her—intending only to wipe the smudge off her chin—she beat a hasty retreat to the doorway. "I'm off to bed. See you in the morning."

"Good night." Drew raised a hand in what he hoped was a good-bye.

As Alexa stepped into the hall, her womanly hourglass shape was silhouetted by the light behind her. She still had all the curves he remembered.

Drew could have smacked himself. That wasn't a helpful observation. Still, he had to check himself to keep from following her down the hall under the lame excuse of checking to make sure she had enough blankets. Alexa wouldn't appreciate his hovering, especially with her stalker situation giving her the willies.

He did allow himself to putter around, double-checking the house's security and getting things ready for the morning before going up to bed. Lingering downstairs also allowed him to keep an ear out in case Alexa needed anything. He'd forgotten to tell her where his room was in case she had a question, but she could probably guess it was upstairs.

He rinsed the coffeepot and wiped it dry. When Granddad died, he'd left the house clean of everything but the big furniture. Personal belongings had been kept by Granddad's secretary at the college and passed out to Drew and his cousins according to the will. The house, with its furniture and library of books, had been left to Drew. His cousins had been compensated for their portion of what the house would have sold for.

When Drew had moved in, he'd been grateful that Granddad left him a house that was ready to be lived in. The place had been a bit dusty since Granddad had passed away almost a year before Dad, and Drew hadn't taken possession until several months after his father's funeral.

The guest room where Alexa was staying had been Drew's room during his visits. When he'd painted the rooms and rearranged the furniture, it had seemed appropriate to hang his father's photos in that room. Now they would keep Alexa company.

The door to the guest bedroom opened, and a moment later, the shower started. Drew listened to the smooth sound of running water and tried to keep images of Alexa, naked with hot water running over her body, out of his head. He remembered her skin being incredibly smooth, and her hair turned dark in the water, making a sharper contrast against her fair skin. The spray would form tiny beads on her breasts—

Drew reined in his thoughts and headed upstairs to his own room. Time for a little distraction before he drove himself crazy.

The watcher curled his lip in bitter amusement as he peered through the brightly lit window. On the other side of the glass pane, Keri was dressed in panties and a thin white top, combing out her long black hair. She was obviously quite vain about her silky tresses, and the watcher considered slipping into her house while she slept and cutting her hair off, just to teach her a lesson. Perhaps he could mark up her face a bit too. Women needed constant supervision, or they got above themselves, and this woman seemed to think she had something Alexa didn't.

But the project didn't hold his interest.

Where was that chit Alexa? She obviously wasn't with Keri. He'd observed her house for long enough to be sure. And if Alexa wasn't staying with her beanpole friend, where was the little pigeon hiding?

He should have stuck around after drowning her cats. But he'd hurried home, so he would be there when Alexa called him after she found the dead kitties. He was a neighbor, of sorts, and he had land where they could be buried. She should have called him.

Instead, his plan had gotten messed up when one of the kittens escaped. Then Alexa had disappeared. But he would find her. There were only so many places she could run. And when he found her, he would fix her good. No more of this idiotic independence thing. She needed a strong man in her life to remind her of her place, which she'd been forgetting. It would be unpleasant for her, but Alexa would be getting what she deserved. Could he help it if he enjoyed being the one to give it to her?

CHAPTER EIGHT

A LEXA WOKE WITH SUNSHINE AND shade in a leafy pattern on her face. It took her a minute to orient herself. She was at Drew's house in the guest bedroom. The clock read almost eight, so she'd really slept in.

Rolling onto her back, she looked around at the photos on the walls and smiled. Her dream last night had been... interesting. She'd missed her fur babies when she'd gone to bed, and she worried about how the cats were doing. But the dream she'd woken up from was all about Drew. He'd been cooking in the kitchen, but he was bare-chested, and the whole scene had been doused in rich sunset colors. Her mind had played it out in slow motion. Every movement of his strong arms and every ripple of his muscles had been painted in lurid crimson and gold. She could almost smell the tangy scent of him and feel the heat that radiated off of him, just like the rays from the sun. Who knew she had such an imagination?

Sounds from the kitchen reminded Alexa that time was passing, and she pushed her dream aside. Fantasies were all very well in the night, but she had a long day ahead of her and didn't need to be blushing every time Drew made eye contact.

She rolled out of bed and grabbed her bathroom bag. When her foot touched the floor, she winced. But with each step afterward, it loosened up and hurt less. Maybe she could do a bit of gentle sparring today. There was no doubt that working out would be good for her soul.

In the hallway, she caught the invigorating aroma of rich coffee, so she hurried through her morning ritual. The coffee smelled divine, and she didn't want to give herself time to fret over how much makeup to wear or how to do her hair. What exactly was the right look when one's day included a touch of sweaty sparring, an interview with a police detective, and plenty of time spent with an old lover turned benign enemy and rescuer? Oh, and she didn't want to forget that she was finishing the day off at the library to get a jump on sorting the donations.

Back in the bedroom, Alexa pulled on a nice pair of slacks that she trusted wouldn't wrinkle and her favorite turquoise sweater. She'd left her sparring uniform at Crouching Tiger the night before, so she would have to change there. She added a pair of dangly earrings made of polished stone, which she'd picked up at a Saturday street festival. Slipping on a pair of comfortable mules that wouldn't bother her scraped foot, she followed the scent of coffee into the kitchen.

Drew was whisking eggs and looked up with a grin when she walked in. He glanced at the clock then back at Alexa. "Good timing. Your omelet has to go on now if it's gonna be cooked in time for you to eat it before your sparring class. You saved yourself from my creative use of fillers."

"Oh, okay, thanks." Alexa glanced over the array of fillers sitting beside the cooktop, feeling incredibly spoiled. Drew's ability to cook had been a total surprise, and she dared not dwell on how she felt about it—or how she felt about her dream. "I'll have broccoli, spinach, tomatoes, and the cheese blend." She poured herself a cup of coffee then turned back to face Drew. "And good morning."

"Good morning." Drew turned his slow smile on her, the one that left her insides melting, while the rest of her felt as though a burst of butterflies were fluttering in every direction. Maybe it was the residual effects of her dream, but this time, Alexa held his chocolate-brown eyes and gave him a slow smile in return.

When Drew was the first to break the look, Alexa felt a smug grin tugging at her lips and lowered her eyes to her mug. Okay, so maybe he just wanted to keep her omelet from burning, but she felt powerful, sensual, in a way she hadn't for a long time... maybe not since she was last with Drew.

Shaking off that thought, Alexa pulled out her cell and went to sit at the kitchen table. She needed to call the vet and see how her kitties were doing. And okay, maybe she needed to think about something that wasn't Drew.

Dr. Springer was happy to launch into a full report on the cats. Drew set Alexa's omelet in front of her, and she nodded her thanks, but her attention was on her conversation with the vet. Oreo and Ragbag were doing great and eating normally, but Fieldgar was struggling to throw off the combined effects of the sleeping medicine and a cold from the water. He'd eaten more of the medicine than the others and had a more sluggish metabolism. Dr. Springer was hopeful that he would improve during the day, but he needed to be kept for observation. He suggested that Alexa leave all the cats a little longer. He thought that keeping Oreo and Ragbag as company would help Fieldgar reach a full recovery.

Alexa agreed that was best and promised to check in again later in the day. She hung up and started on her omelet. The eggs were fluffy, and the veggies were cooked just right. Her heart and stomach were grateful for the simple comfort as her mind turned over the phone call. Dr. Springer had sounded optimistic and upbeat, but underneath his words were the things not said. Fieldgar had experienced a serious overdose, and it was possible he wouldn't recover.

A warm, strong hand slipped over hers, and Alexa looked up to see Drew watching her.

"They'll be okay," he said gently. "Dr. Springer would tell you if there was any real concern. He would have you come in so you could be there if things went south. The cats will be okay."

Tears sprang to Alexa's eyes at this unexpected comfort, but she blinked them away and smiled shakily. "You're right. Fieldgar's just a big cat and taking a little longer. I'm sure they'll all be okay."

Drew gave her hand a little squeeze of encouragement then gathered their plates and rinsed them. A few minutes of tidying later, and they were ready to head into town. Alexa gulped down the last of her coffee and grabbed her purse.

"So, why Fieldgar?" Drew asked as he started up the truck. "I'm not up on cat names, but isn't that one a bit unusual?"

"It's actually taken from the name of a highly famous cat that I'm sure you're very familiar with." Alexa chuckled at Drew's puzzled face. "Garfield, the comic strip cat. I just gave his name a tweak. Fieldgar looks like his famous friend, and eats like him, but unlike Garfield, he's got a sweet disposition and a generous heart."

"Ergo, Fieldgar," Drew said with an appreciative laugh. "I like it. I look forward to getting to know him better."

Alexa smiled, comforted by their shared good humor. But as she settled back in her seat, her mind replayed Drew's last sentence. Did he just assume they would see the cats sometime before the stalker left them free to go their separate ways, or was he suggesting that they would continue as friends after the danger had passed? Did he want to start seeing Alexa in a romantic way? And how would she react if he did?

Drew was quiet as he drove through town, and Alexa watched him while pretending not to. Today, he was wearing a close-knit turtleneck, with a blazer-style jacket over it. He looked good—too good for her peace of mind.

At least she no longer wanted to grind his face in the dirt and stomp on it. It was hard to maintain that level of animosity toward someone who fed her good food, took her in when she needed a safe haven, and offered comfort when she was sad. But despite all that, she still didn't trust him as a boyfriend. She really, really didn't trust him as a boyfriend. And she wasn't sure she cared for him as a person, either. How did she even know his motives in taking her in were altruistic? Didn't Rangers go after their objectives by any means? So why not butter Alexa up by being the white knight in exchange for her promoting goodwill toward his MMA club? But if that was his reason for turning into Mr. Nice Guy, how would she know?

When Alexa left sparring, she was tired and sticky with sweat, limping a bit on her aching foot, but she was thoroughly calm. That was one reason she loved martial arts. When it came to burning off excess energy and angst, it was the next best thing to sex. And she hadn't had any of that since moving back to Willowdale after finishing her library science degree. Sparring was not only easier to come by, it was much, much safer.

When the last sparring class was dismissed, Alexa looked up to see Detective Rawlings standing by the office door. The detective had watched her sons' sparring class, and she was dressed in jeans and a sweater. She lifted her checkbook at Alexa then smiled and nodded toward the office.

Alexa excused herself to the other black belts and followed Detective Rawlings into the office, closing the door behind her. "I'm assuming that was your very subtle way of saying we need to talk?"

Detective Rawlings smiled. "You guessed it, but I really do need to make a tuition payment as well. Would you mind looking up what I owe while I fill you in?"

Alexa nodded and slipped behind the desk so she could pull up the tuition accounts on the computer. She pushed aside the orange candle to make room.

"That's the candle left by the stalker?" Detective Rawlings leaned in for a closer look.

"I'm guessing it was left by him," Alexa answered. "It was the first item left for me and had no note beyond my name in gold glitter."

Detective Rawlings nodded and sat back after inspecting the candle. "It's looks to be a generic make and seems unexceptional beyond the personalization, which was done after purchase. Probably dozens of fingerprints, too, since it's been sitting in this office. All the same, I'll send one of the guys by to pick it up sometime when no one is around to notice it being carted off. I'd rather not alert anyone here that we're suspicious."

Alexa looked up from the computer. "Does that mean you believe the stalker comes to Crouching Tiger?"

"Not necessarily." Detective Rawlings shook her head. "We still need to get a list of guys you've dated, and consider other possible angles. And additionally, we can't dismiss the possibility that Jason Stone has come back, probably motivated by revenge. It's my instinct that stalking you isn't his style, but he was released from prison in April."

Alexa froze, her muscles going rigid. "He's out? And has been free for six months? But he hasn't finished his sentence!"

Detective Rawlings spoke in a soothing tone. "His sentence was reduced, which is common enough. However, I'm checking with his parole officer, and we'll keep careful tabs on his whereabouts." She lifted a calming hand. "I promise that we will take every precaution, and I'll give Drew his description, but I don't believe he's our best suspect."

Alexa blew out the breath she'd been holding. "Okay, I guess. I mean, it's been years, and he lives most of the way across the country. Plus, surely I'd have recognized him if he was hanging around town."

"There you go," Detective Rawlings said. "Until I hear back from his parole officer, we'll move on with the possible candidates from right here in Willowdale. The situation with the keys points toward someone who could move freely within Crouching Tiger, which unfortunately leaves us with a large pool of suspects. For that reason and others, I'd prefer we keep things quiet and discreet until we have a better sense of what we're up against."

Alexa nodded. "Fine by me." She glanced at the computer, which was beeping a warning that she would be logged out if she continued to ignore it. "You had a credit on your account but still owe sixty-eight dollars for this month's tuition for your boys."

"Great, thanks." Detective Rawlings wrote out a check for the amount and passed it over to Alexa. "Given the need for discretion, I'd rather not fingerprint you here. Too many curious people. Is there somewhere else that comes to mind, or would you rather come down to the station?"

"How about the library?" Alexa asked. "I'm not working circulation today, just stopping in to do some sorting. We could talk in one of the back rooms, and no one would be the wiser."

"Sounds perfect." Detective Rawlings stood up. "I'll meet you there in, say, half an hour?"

Alexa nodded. "I'll be there." She followed Detective Rawlings out of the office then headed back for a quick shower in the women's changing room. As she walked through the dojo, she texted Drew's cell and asked him to meet them at the library. He offered to pick her up, but she said no. The library was a public place, and no one would think anything about Drew being there. But if they arrived together, someone would notice. Besides, he was her ride back to his house—not her babysitter.

Keri caught up to Alexa at the door to the locker room. "Sure you won't change your mind and come party with us?"

Alexa shook her head. "No, I have to put in some time at the library. But if you could give me a minute to clean up, I'll let you give me a ride over there and claim my staff parking spot. Best possible parking for the festival!"

Keri laughed. "Done and done. Just come to the lobby when you're ready."

Alexa nodded and hurried to get cleaned up.

CHAPTER NINE

A N HOUR LATER, IN A back room of the library, Alexa sat across from Detective Rawlings with several boxes of books beside her. "So that's it," Alexa said. "I haven't been on any other dates. Unless you count an outing this summer with Brian, Stuart, and Keri, but that was really a group thing." She picked up another book from the stack in front of her and put it in the box that would go on the table of two-dollar books.

Detective Rawlings leaned back in her chair and tapped the paper in front of her with her pen. "And none of these men were more important than any other? You weren't intimately involved with any of them?"

Alexa shrugged. "Not unless you're counting a good-night kiss as intimacy. And that was only once, with the middle school teacher, Henry Dower. He got further than any of the others, but his kiss was more of a peck, anyway." She pulled the next book from the box—a romance with a rich red cover and a couple locked in an intimate embrace. She sighed and tossed the book into the two-dollar box.

"Pathetic, isn't it?" Alexa asked. "Between my work at Crouching Tiger and this library, I know just about everyone in town. I'm young, available, and reasonably attractive. But my love life as listed on that paper"—Alexa waved her hand at the sheet in front of Detective Rawlings—"aspires to the heady passions of a classic spinster librarian."

Detective Rawlings smiled. "It's not a long list, but it sounds like you've turned down more dates than you've said yes to. That doesn't mean there's anything wrong with you. It means you don't want to date." She glanced at the open door Drew had passed through. He was reading a book and hovering just out of earshot. "You're sure there isn't anyone else?" she asked carefully. "Anyone who may feel they have a prior claim on you, or that you've been..." She paused, seeming to search for the right word.

"I've been waiting for? Keeping myself for?" Alexa was quiet for a minute. "No one that needs to go on the suspect list."

Detective Rawlings nodded, her smile sympathetic. "Well, then," she said briskly. "Let's get on with the fingerprinting. I've got enough information here to do background checks and ask a few questions. Our profiler is putting something together that may help."

Alexa nodded her thanks and quickly sorted the last of the books in the donation box.

Detective Rawlings stuck her head out and waved Drew over. "Once we get Alexa fingerprinted, her fingers will have ink stains, so I'd like the two of you to leave quietly from the back door of the library. Fewer questions that way."

Alexa followed Detective Rawlings's instructions and carefully rolled her finger over the ink pad before transferring the print onto a card the detective had supplied. Drew stood beside her and watched, which made it hard to concentrate. She tried to focus on getting clear prints and was relieved when she was finished and could step away from Drew.

Detective Rawlings lifted Alexa's fingerprints and looked them over before setting the paper aside. "Looks clear. I've already pulled yours, Drew."

"I'm a little surprised I wasn't fingerprinted when I started at the library." Alexa looked at Drew. "I'm guessing you were fingerprinted a long time ago? Rangers have clearance, don't they?"

"I was printed as a recruit, actually," Drew said. "But I'm guessing the prints the police have are more current—the ones from when I moved back here and applied for my concealed-carry permit."

Detective Rawlings nodded. "Those are the ones on file. Now that we have both sets, we'll eliminate your prints so we can isolate the stalker's, if there are any. Let's hope he wasn't savvy enough to wear gloves."

Alexa nodded and forced a smile, but she found that dwelling on the stalker roaming through her house just made her sick.

She held her hands up. "Mind if I go quickly wash? There's a sink back here in the staff lounge."

The detective nodded, and Alexa left Detective Rawlings and Drew chatting about different fingerprint-dusting techniques and why the local police hadn't purchased a portable electronic biometric scanner.

Alexa scrubbed her hands quickly, thinking of her fur babies as she did. It was time she checked in to see how they were doing. Once her hands were clean and dry, albeit still ink stained, she headed for the big utility door at the back of the library. There was a courtyard garden behind the library, where she could wait for Drew and make her call without being overheard.

Just as she opened the big metal door, she heard Drew call her name and looked back.

Drew walked swiftly toward her, concern on his face. "What are you doing, going off by yourself? If you need—"

Alexa made a sharp shushing motion with her hand. No one was supposed to know they were friends now or see them together, but they would be sure to figure it out if he kept after her like that. What was he thinking?

Alexa let go of the big door and stepped back toward Drew.

The door slammed shut. A sharp crash came from the other side of it.

Drew was at Alexa's side in an instant, pushing her against the wall and shielding her with his body from anyone who might come through the door. He pulled a gun from the holster hidden underneath his jacket

Alexa held her breath, her heart beating a crazy pitter-patter. *Please let it just be a stray dog or the wind blowing something over.* It was strange—this queasy adrenaline rush felt nothing like the heady rush she got from sparring. She couldn't take her eyes off of Drew's gun.

He silently signaled for Alexa to pull the door open but stay hidden behind it.

She put a brake on her racing emotions and quietly did as he asked.

As soon as the door was open, Drew ducked out with his gun held ready.

Drew came back in. His was face grim, but his gun was pointed down in a more relaxed stance. "Get Detective Rawlings."

Alexa let her breath out in a rush. "Is someone out there?"

Drew shook his head. "I didn't see anyone, but I think your stalker was there."

That was enough to send Alexa hurrying in search of Detective Rawlings. She found the detective browsing in the kids' section. Alexa didn't have to say a word. Apparently, her face said it all. The detective dropped her books on the shelf and followed Alexa. Neither of them spoke until they were in the staff section again.

"What's the situation?" Detective Rawlings asked. "Did your stalker make a move?"

"It looks like it." Alexa didn't want to tell the detective she hadn't seen what had happened and didn't know what was going on. Once again, her life was spiraling out of control, but this time, all her fears seemed justified.

When they reached Drew, he pulled the door open wide, and the women looked out at the small brick courtyard. On the bricks right outside the door was a mess of shattered glass, jumbled books, and broken pottery.

Detective Rawlings pulled gloves from her coat pocket and stepped out gingerly. Avoiding the glass as best she could, she examined the scene. She pointed to the wall beside the door. "The light has been broken. Alexa, where are these books from?"

Alexa stepped forward and leaned out to get a better look at the books and pottery, wincing as she put weight on her sore foot. It was almost all better, but it still complained if she stepped wrong. "They're all from the reference section on the second floor, and I think"—she leaned down to examine the pattern on a bigger shard of pottery—"this is one of the urns from upstairs." She shook her head and stepped back so Detective Rawlings could come back inside. "Ms. Tullep is going to be brokenhearted. She loves those urns."

"If the stalker is still here, we may have bigger problems than Ms. Tullep's urn."

Detective Rawlings flipped open her cell phone and spoke quickly to someone as she walked toward the front of the library. She stopped at the staff gate and looked back. "Can the two of you tuck yourselves out of sight for a few minutes, 'til we know what's up? I don't want you seen together, but I need you to stay here."

Alexa nodded and led Drew into Ms. Tullep's office. The initial sick feeling of shock was wearing off, leaving her feeling a bit breathless but very alert. She closed the door behind them and locked it. "Ms. Tullep isn't in today. She never works Saturdays. No one will disturb us here." As soon as the words were out of her mouth, she realized how intimate they sounded, and heat rose in her cheeks.

Drew flashed her a grin, but his mind seemed to be elsewhere. He prowled around the confined space, looking at pictures on the walls and glancing over shelves. He stopped in front of Alexa. "When you opened the door, did you see anyone out there?"

She shook her head.

"Which would be unlikely, given that the books appear to have been dropped from the second floor," Drew said. "Is there a window over that door?"

Alexa closed her eyes, trying to picture the back of the building, then shook her head. She opened her eyes and crossed to Ms. Tullep's desk. "Somewhere around here, there are framed before and after pictures, from when the old florist shop was converted into our library. It might show the placement of the windows."

Drew helped her look, and in a few minutes, they were bending over the paired pictures. To the left was the grainy black-and-white photograph taken when the building served as Rose's Flowers. On the right was a glossy picture of the library eight years ago when the conversion was completed.

Alexa pointed to the back door and the window just above it. "Not directly over it, but only off by a few inches."

"What's this?" Drew pointed to a skinny beam sticking out from the back wall of the building.

"Just something left over from the floral shop." Alexa wiped a finger around the frame, clearing away dust. "I think it was used to hang long banners and sometimes flower arrangements."

A knock sounded at the door.

Drew quickly took up a position on the side of the door, his hand on his gun in its underarm holster.

Alexa waited until he was ready then leaned close to the door. "Who is it?"

"Detective Rawlings."

She opened the door, and the detective came in.

"We searched the building but didn't find a likely suspect," Detective Rawlings said. "Most of your patrons are older people or moms with kids. There was a young couple getting a little too affectionate in the poetry section and a group of teen boys that the deputy is questioning, but I doubt anything will come of it."

Drew crossed to the desk. "I don't think he dropped the pot when he heard the door open. He would have needed to sprint to get out of the library fast enough." Drew tapped the photo. "I'm thinking he perched the pot with the books in it on this beam."

Detective Rawlings peered at the picture and nodded. "That makes sense. If he balanced the urn on the beam, the force of the door slamming would shake the beam, and the urn would fall."

Drew nodded. "Exactly."

"You mean…" Alexa's voice was a little squeaky. "He set it up then just left it there?"

Detective Rawlings nodded absently. She took the photo from Drew and looked it over closely. "We'll check it out. Good thinking, Drew."

"But if that's what he did…" Alexa shook her head. "That would mean whoever next used that door would get hit on the head with a falling clay pot and several thick reference books. Not to mention broken glass because it broke the light. Anyone who used the door, not just me!"

Detective Rawlings and Drew exchanged a look. "It looks that way," Detective Rawlings said carefully.

A wave of nausea washed over Alexa. The adrenaline she'd been running on crested and left her feeling a buzzy alarm that bordered on paranoia. The combined weight of the books and pot must have been really heavy and would have hit with a lot of force, possibly enough force to kill someone. And the trap had been set indiscriminately, so any of the library staff could have been hurt. Just what was this guy willing to do to hurt her?

Drew rested his hand on Alexa's shoulder and spoke to the detective. "If there's nothing more, I think it's time we go."

"Yes, good idea," Detective Rawlings agreed. "I'll let you know what we find."

Mentally collecting herself, Alexa rose and offered Detective Rawlings her hand. "Thanks for all your help."

The detective nodded and shook Alexa's hand. "Just take care of yourself and stick close to Drew. Do that, and you'll be okay."

Alexa nodded and allowed Drew to lead her out the back door of the library. She couldn't help but cringe and glance away as she stepped over the glass and picked her way through the mess outside the door. A deputy was bent down, taking pictures. He nodded as they walked by but said nothing. Luckily, the small back garden was sheltered from the road, and the near-accident hadn't attracted any attention.

When she was buckled into Drew's truck, Alexa leaned back and wrapped her arms around herself. The level of casual violence this sicko had shown left her shivering somewhere deep inside.

"The detective didn't mention any leads, did she?" Alexa asked, turning to Drew.

He shook his head. "No, she didn't say."

Alexa's gaze went to her beloved little town, and her voice came out ragged. "So, we have no idea who this man is. How could I have unwittingly inspired that kind of hatred and anger in someone I can't even put a face to? Unless this is all the work of Jason Stone, and he's come back to make me pay?"

"I'll be interested to see what the profiler comes up with, but I don't think it was him." Drew's tone was thoughtful. "From what you said, he acted impulsively when he attacked your friend and was very direct. This fellow seems super sneaky, and so far, I think he's mostly intended to scare you."

"You think so? Those bricks in that pot could have killed me." Her voice wobbled a bit on the end of the sentence.

Drew gave her a sympathetic look. "Could have, but the pot fell to the outside, away from the door, so a direct hit was unlikely."

Alexa thought about that, but it wasn't as comforting as Drew meant it to be. She still would have been badly banged up or super scared, no matter what. And having two men out there who might want her dead wasn't a happy thought. "Maybe Jason Stone's tactics have changed. He spent more than three years in prison."

"That's possible." Drew reached over with his free hand and briefly cupped Alexa's hand in his. "Whoever it is, the detective will figure it out. I'm sure of it."

Alexa nodded, swallowing around the tightness in her throat.

Drew made a left turn off the main road, and Alexa frowned. "This isn't the way we went to your house last time, is it?" Was he afraid they were being followed? She looked behind the truck but didn't see anyone.

"We're making a stop on the way." Drew gave her a half grin that dispelled her worries, but he still didn't tell her where they were going.

He cut through a grocery store parking lot then parked. "Do you recognize where we are?"

Alexa nodded, warmth and gratitude swelling up inside her as she did. Her brain hadn't been keeping up with his unusual route, but they were in the back parking lot of Dr. Springer's veterinary clinic.

Drew came around the truck and helped her out then walked with her toward the door. "Dr. Springer said to come to the back door. He'll have the cats ready to come home."

"Wait." Alexa stopped in her tracks. "When did you have the chance to talk to him?"

"I didn't." Drew's grin grew wider. "I texted him when we left the library. I figured you could use a happy reunion."

Alexa didn't think—she just acted on impulse, and the next second, she was standing there with her arms around Drew. It was just so sweet of him to think of that, and he was right that she really needed to be with her cats.

Standing in his arms, she was suddenly very aware of his broad chest, tight abs, and the protective circle of his arms around her. His scent somehow always smelled fresh, as if he were soaked in sunshine.

She'd enjoyed the company of men before, Drew's in particular, but this was different. She felt as though her body and soul were asking to wed this man, to be his and have him by her in a much more intimate way than even sex.

The feeling released a heady rush of hormones that swept all thought away. She could lose herself in Drew's warmth and kisses. In his arms, she would have no worries, only bliss. It would feel so good to give herself to him as she had before.

Thankfully, that "as she had before" thought brought her back to her senses. She was feeling a temporary urge, brought on by fear and a primal need to feel safe. It meant nothing, just as their time together had meant nothing to him.

Alexa stepped out of Drew's arms and tried to hike a smile into place. Her voice was a little wobbly when she spoke. "S-Sorry about that. And thanks for setting this up."

Drew gave a half nod, his face strained as he turned away from her.

Alexa felt her heart pinch for having possibly distressed him but reminded herself that being with Drew was a temporary arrangement. Anything more than that would only lead to heartache.

CHAPTER TEN

DREW LISTENED WITH HALF AN ear to Alexa's conversation with Dr. Springer, but most of his attention was on pulling himself back together.

What was he going to do? He'd been attracted to Alexa since the first time they met. He'd been walking the Saturday street festival with a buddy, and she was running a fundraiser table for her college. He chatted with her then went back when it was time to clean up and helped her pack up her stuff. They walked over to Crazy Pops afterward, and he thought that watching her suck on a Crazy Pop had to be the sexiest thing he'd ever seen.

The rest of his leave was glorious. The three weeks were full of laughter and sizzling-hot sex, plus long walks and romps around the town. Alexa fascinated him. She was a sexy juxtaposition of all that was feminine and lovely set beside a determined independence, like satin over a titanium core. He gave her his full attention while they were together, but once he shipped off, he tried to keep her out of his mind. That mission was his first assignment as a Ranger, and he was determined to stay focused. Besides, things had ended messily between them. She'd called him one evening just at the end of his leave when he was in a fight. It was justified but ugly, and he had been forced to spend time in unsavory company at the police station, where he'd almost been booked. The incident had shaken his confidence to the core, and he didn't want her to know, so when Alexa called, he was short with her, rude. He was just young enough and shortsighted enough to believe he was moving on, and he wanted to keep her from viewing him in an embarrassing light. Alexa sounded terribly hurt. She tried to press him and get him to open up. He'd been afraid for her to know the whole truth but felt terrible about hurting her, which only made him feel like a bigger jerk. He'd ended the call by saying something stupid about her being too needy then hung up. He hadn't returned her calls afterward or acknowledged her once he shipped out.

Now he couldn't remember any part of the incident without disgust. He had initially avoided Alexa when he came back to Willowdale, in part because he felt ashamed of how he'd handled the end of their brief relationship. At first, he'd hoped to find the right moment then have her out for coffee and see if he could smooth things over. But she'd given him so much grief over his school that he soon dropped any notion of making it up to her. Besides, by smearing his name all around town, she'd made him pay for any past wrongs twenty times over.

When she'd hugged him just now, though, he was suddenly aware of a searing fact that he'd managed to ignore all these years. He loved Alexa. He had always loved her.

The fact left him speechless and vulnerable in ways he hadn't been since... he couldn't say when. Only a couple of times in his life even came close. In Ranger school, the instructors had pushed him and all the men past their limits, washing good guys out like refuse. In the deep, dark days when chemo had taken a toll on his father, they'd both begun to realize this was one battle they couldn't win.

But this was different. This feeling of love for her reached deep into the core of his soul. Even scarier, he had no guarantees she would ever love him back. What did he have to offer her? Sure, he was a Ranger, but he knew only too well that some civilians put little stock in that. And anyway, Rangers didn't have great track records when it came to relationships. He'd also done well for himself, and between his own investments and the inherited estate from his father and granddad, he was well enough off. But Alexa was independent and had not only a bachelor's degree, but a master's as well. Even more importantly, she had a refinement and poise to her that gave even her little finger grace.

She could have any guy—even a PhD—and maybe that was what she wanted. The painful past they had between them... what if she never forgave him or loved him back? Did he want to risk his heart to that kind of pain?

He watched Alexa as she smiled and chatted with Dr. Springer. Her arms were cuddled around her cats, and her face glowed with pleasure that they were okay. Drew noticed the sparkle in her eyes and the intelligence in her expression. Clean curves started with the line of her calves and swooped up her figure—as womanly as any guy could ever want—and carried on through the arch of her neck and the way she carried her head. He wanted her, and she would be worth any risk. He knew it.

The challenge was going to be figuring out how to get her to love him back, and not as a summer fling, but for forever. Because if he was going to go after her, he had to do it properly—and first, he had to keep her safe. Second, he had to persuade her to be his willing wife.

<hr>

Alexa was grateful the ride back to Drew's house was short. Ragbag had been cooped up much more than usual over the last forty-eight hours, and he clearly wanted out of the cat carrier. Still, Alexa hesitated to open the carrier the minute she got inside Drew's house. What would he think about having her cats roam all over his place? What if they shredded something priceless that his granddad had left him? The awkwardness of being super polite while staying with him was starting to get under her skin. He was being beyond thoughtful, but she wasn't sure he saw her as herself and not a damsel in distress or an unfortunate civilian in need of a Special Ops rescue. She wasn't some mission he could check off his Ranger to-do list. Perhaps she wasn't being fair to him, but with her emotions all over the place, she longed for a sense of control, to be her own woman again.

Drew came up beside her with the cats' litter box and food in his arms. "Put the litter in the bathroom and the food in the kitchen?"

"Perfect," Alexa answered. Ragbag gave a pathetic meow, pleading to get out of the carrier. Alexa pursed her lips. "My cats are house-trained, but in a new environment, there are always ways for them to get into trouble, and Ragbag is still a kitten. I can't promise—"

"Don't worry about it." Drew shrugged off her concern. "I'll just move anything that becomes a problem to an extra bedroom upstairs and keep the door closed. They'll be fine."

Alexa gave him a grateful smile and opened the carrier. She couldn't deny that it felt good to have someone watching her back like this. Drew could have asked for the cats to stay at the vet, especially since he hadn't signed up to babysit them when he offered to protect her. Instead, he had arranged the cat pickup and was beyond cool about her fur babies running around his house. His attentive care for her cats was sweet and gave her the same cherished feeling she'd had when they dated.

However, she still didn't entirely trust his motives in offering her his protection. She hadn't forgotten how fast he turned from hot to cold five years before. The last thing she needed right now was to make herself vulnerable to possible pain from Drew—not with a twisted psycho trailing her every move.

Remembering the smashing sound of the pot thudding onto the pavement, right where her head should have been, Alexa shivered and felt her skin grow cold. She didn't want to think about it, but it was hard *not* to think about.

Curling up in a patch of sunshine with her back to the couch, Alexa picked up Fieldgar and settled down to cuddle her biggest fur baby. The orange tabby was happy to snuggle. His rumbling purr immediately quieted Alexa's shivers but couldn't quite banish them. Watching the other two cats also helped calm her and brought a smile to her face. Oreo was doing a quick and thorough search of the premises, and Ragbag was frolicking around the black-and-white kitty, pointing out anything Oreo might have missed. After they'd made a circuit of the living room, kitchen, and dining room, they stopped in front of the closed French doors on the far side of the dining room and meowed at Alexa to open them up.

She followed them but glanced around for Drew. This was the entrance to the second wing, on the opposite side of the house from the guest bedroom. She hadn't been in there yet.

"Go ahead. Open it up," Drew said, coming through the kitchen to join them. "That's the library. I'm betting your cats will like it."

Alexa swung the doors open and stepped in then flicked on a light. What she saw made her suck in a breath and clutch Fieldgar to her chest. It looked like heaven.

The entire wing was one big room, and every wall was lined with beautiful dark bookcases that were filled with books. She'd never seen so many books collected in one place outside of a public library.

Across from her was a brick fireplace and hearth with a love seat and two cozy chairs gathered around it. Sunshine spilled through a pair of patio doors to her right, begging readers to bring a book out and enjoy the sweet little garden she'd seen at the front of the house. It was beautiful—the library of her dreams.

Drew spoke close beside her, his deep voice resonating along her skin. "Shall I get a fire going?"

She nodded, unwilling to trust her voice. The combination of this beautiful library and its sexy owner was just a tad overpowering. She set Fieldgar down and walked farther into the room, browsing along the shelves and smiling when she came across old favorites among the books. She found the collected works of Shakespeare and *The Canterbury Tales*. But the library didn't just have the classics. It also had a nice collection of modern fiction novels, ranging from James Paterson thrillers to the Harry Potter books and beyond. She had finished one full circuit by the time Drew had the hearth blazing merrily. She'd gathered a small stack of books to look at too.

Alexa curled up on the love seat beside Oreo, who was watching the flames flicker in the fire. This was nice—and just what her soul needed. "You have a wonderful variety of books," she told Drew. "Most people who collect books in a library of this kind only go for the classics and their prestigious peers in nonfiction."

Drew grinned and nudged a log farther into the fire, sending sparks flying. He'd shed his jacket and tugged up the sleeves on his deep-blue turtleneck. "Granddad collected the traditional library fare, but he was also happy to get any books his grandkids wanted to read. I've used his method in choosing more."

"And these books? Who added these to the collection?" Alexa held up two of the books she'd found while wandering around the room. The first was *Quintessence of Japanese Martial Arts*, and the second was *The Ancient Martial Arts: A Guide for the Purist.*

"Ah, you found my secret stash." Drew got up from the fireplace and sat beside her on the love seat. He picked up Oreo then resettled her in his lap and started tickling the cat's chin. "Granddad got the Japanese book for me when I was a teen. I was taking karate and wanted to know more about its history. He knew Dad's orders would change soon, and that it would mean my leaving the karate school before I could get my black belt. He was hoping staying here over Christmas and studying that book would soften my disappointment."

Alexa pulled her eyes away from the hypnotic motion of Drew's hand as he stroked Oreo, and met his eyes. She didn't know Drew had ever studied the traditional martial arts. "Did it work?"

He shrugged. "Yeah, it helped. The focus of the ancient martial arts was on enlightenment and mastery, not rank advancement. Then I realized that I didn't care quite so much about getting the formal rank of black belt."

That also might explain his casual approach to a formal martial arts school, but Alexa didn't feel like picking a fight with him at that moment.

Oreo stretched out and purred loud enough for Alexa to feel the vibration through the love seat. The kitty caught Drew's hand with her paws and gave it a thorough cleaning. Drew tugged his hand free and laid his arm across the back of the seat, behind Alexa's shoulders.

It was such a classic date move—a guy wanting to put his arm around a girl but not sure he could. Alexa would have laughed if it weren't for the breathless combination of hormone flutters and nerves she felt at having him so close that made her heart speed up. She made a conscious decision to slow down her breathing. Drew wasn't putting any moves on her. They were just talking.

She forced herself to look back at him, despite the mesmerizing effect of his eyes. "So, what about the other book? I wouldn't have pegged you as a purist."

Drew smiled, and she was torn between listening to his response and noticing how close his fingers—the ones petting the cat—were coming to her stockinged foot. "That's a recent addition. Just because I don't follow the traditional arts, doesn't mean I can't learn from them."

Alexa swallowed and twitched her foot out of Drew's reach. "So, you don't—" Her breath caught behind her teeth.

Drew had captured her foot—the one that hadn't been banged up—in his hands and was gently massaging the ball. "Your foot was twitching." He sounded almost apologetic.

She decided not to mention that it was twitching away from him, especially not when his hands felt so good as they soothed the tension from her poor toes.

He was looking down at her foot, so she had a moment to enjoy his profile—his firm but sensuous lips, a good nose and forehead. Why had she never noticed before how intellectual he looked? She'd been thinking all these years of Drew as a thorough military man, all action and solid muscle. How had she missed the side of him that framed his father's photography, whipped up a gourmet meal, and made regular additions to his grandfather's library?

She felt something shift inside of her, possibly in the area around her heart, and tried desperately to backtrack onto safe ground. "You don't have a problem with traditional martial arts?" she asked, her voice coming out a bit huskier than she expected.

Drew glanced up at her and flashed her one of those grins he had, the kind that melted her insides and left her feeling like a breathless schoolgirl. The warm look in his eyes, the way the sweater accentuated his sculpted chest and broad shoulders, coupled with the insistent massaging of his hands… did he know what he was doing to her?

"I know you'll have a hard time believing this," Drew was saying. "But I support the traditional martial arts. I've studied most of the forms, at least a little, and they all have value." His fingers shifted to work down Alexa's foot, making a gentle circular motion on the arch, and she had to bite her lip to keep in a moan. "I can't set up a school in the traditional arts because my highest rank is brown belt. It's also my belief that much of what we need today in order to practice effective self-defense is a blending of the traditional arts. I want what I teach to be directly applicable to my students' lives."

His fingers captured her other foot, carefully avoiding the sore area on top, and gently prodded at a tight spot on the underside. Alexa tried to pull her brain back into focus, but it felt a lot like trying to roll out of a warm bed on a chilly morning.

Her lips parted, but no words came out. Her eyes settled on Drew's lips. She would give just about anything to kiss him, to taste his tongue against hers, feel their mouths locked together while her body was enveloped by his.

Drew looked up to meet her gaze, and the intellectual profile was replaced by a sexy, smoldering look. She knew he wanted to kiss her too.

He brought his hand up to trail across her hair, soothing it, then he let it slide down to cup her jaw. Dimly, Alexa was aware of alarm bells going off in the back of her brain, but their sound was muted by the thudding of her heart. Drew leaned in, his deep-brown eyes intent on hers. His lips parted, and their shared breath mingled.

The fire popped—the sound like a gunshot in the quiet room.

Alexa jumped, her body buzzing with nervous anxiety. She slid quickly away from Drew and stood.

Ragbag was checking something out on the floor by the fire, his body in a half crouch. He reached out a paw to bat at whatever it was then jerked his paw back. Alexa saw a wink of red ember.

"Silly kitty," she said, going to him. "Keep playing with that, and you're going to get burned."

She swept up the ember and tossed it back in the fire then turned to face Drew. He sat with his arms stretched out along the back of the couch, his head tilted up to her. He looked so damned sexy—her body ached to join him. But the words she'd spoken just a moment ago to Ragbag circled through her brain. Play with that, and she was just going to get burned.

Alexa wrapped her arms around herself, keeping her feelings in. "Well, I'm off for bed." The cheerful voice she was going for came out a little too forced, and she modulated it to a more normal tone. "Thanks for helping with the cats and for being cool with their coming here. I really appreciate it."

Drew nodded, his shoulders making a small shrug. "They're welcome anytime, just as you are."

Alexa just stood there, not sure how to respond, not sure if she trusted herself. How had she gone from hating this man to almost kissing him in two days?

Drew rose, his body moving with the same fluid grace she'd admired when he changed her tire. He spoke pleasantly, as if they hadn't been inches apart just moments ago. "I set out food and water for the cats in the kitchen. Do they need anything else?"

She shook her head. "No, they'll be fine."

"Do you need anything?" Drew closed the screen on the fireplace. "I could throw together a bedtime snack if you like."

A flippant comment about him as her bedtime snack flitted across Alexa's brain, but she shook the thought aside. Next, she would be offering him the keys to Crouching Tiger and asking if he would like her to pose naked on the floor of the dojo. Speaking of which, what was that he'd said when he was distracting her with a foot massage? About wanting what he taught to have practical use in his students' lives?

She felt her face heat with anger this time instead of hormones. His statement was out of line, implying that Crouching Tiger didn't teach skills with practical uses in students' lives! He'd just snuck in that bit of brainwashing while she was distracted and wouldn't protest, hadn't he? Was that his game? Because the more she thought about it, the more she suspected he was using her, or at least playing with her. He had to have known what he was doing when he touched her foot like that. Next, he would be asking her to help with his school open house, and that would be the end of her having a mind of her own where martial arts were concerned.

He finished with the fire and turned toward her, a questioning look on his face, and she realized she still hadn't answered him. He probably thought she was considering an invitation to her bed. *Not!*

"I'm fine, thanks." Her voice was flat and cold. She bent to scoop up Ragbag and headed out of the room before she could say something she would regret. Oreo and Fieldgar followed her from the library and trailed her across the house to the guest bedroom.

The room was a bit chilly, so Alexa pulled an extra blanket off the stack in the closet and spread it over the bed. Her body ached for a more satisfying way to warm the bed, but the quilt would do. She'd come close to falling under Drew's spell. This beautiful house and its cozy rooms were just the right backdrop, and he was turning on all his charms.

She snorted. He could probably talk a girl right into his bed without her even knowing how she'd gotten there. The more attractive she found Drew, the more watchful she needed to be in keeping up her guard. Because no way was she going to survive her stalker only to find herself as Drew's sweet and gullible girlfriend.

CHAPTER ELEVEN

THE NEXT MORNING ALEXA GOT up and hopped in the shower early, even though it was Sunday. Every time she'd fallen asleep during the night, her dreams had alternated between hot, steamy affairs focused on Drew, and psychedelic nightmares in which a faceless madman hunted her and everyone she loved. Worst were the ones that came closest to real life, where she found herself making love to Drew, only to look up and see a man's eyes watching her through the window. Those dreams were not only horrible, but they were an excellent message from her psyche that this was not the time to get involved with Drew, even if she'd wanted to.

Clearly, her overwrought brain needed something to focus on besides her two hot-button topics. Moreover, something she definitely did not need was Drew making her another sumptuous breakfast. She resisted the urge to primp, opting for the light makeup she usually wore to work. She pulled her hair back from her face in two clips, then she slipped out of her room and went hunting breakfast.

After five minutes of scrounging in the cupboards, she settled on cold cereal. Then she plunked herself down at the kitchen table to eat and pretend to read *Martial Arts Monthly*. She kept an ear out to track Drew's progress upstairs, so she wasn't taken by surprise when he came into the kitchen. He looked fresh and fantastic in a pair of slacks and a collared polo shirt.

"Good morning." She watched him over her magazine as he puttered about, getting himself coffee.

He smiled at her. "Good morning. I see you found breakfast."

She only nodded, pretending to be engrossed in her article. There was nothing wrong with their conversation, but she was still embarrassed. It would have sounded much the same if they'd spent the night together.

He cleared her empty bowl without being asked, and she caught a hint of his aftershave. Her nostrils flared at the musky scent that held some kind of spice, cedar maybe, which she'd noticed before. It fit him perfectly, and he smelled divine.

Alexa dropped her magazine and stood up. Time to get something productive done, like... The trouble was she didn't have a lot she could do there. The library donation boxes were all either at the library or at her house, and she wasn't scheduled to work. There weren't any classes at Crouching Tiger since it was Sunday. And her usual errands would take her out in public—with Drew. Even worse, her foot was close to one hundred percent, so her body was urging her to do something active. She roamed about, picking up after the kitties and tidying up.

Drew stepped in front of her, placing both hands gently on her shoulders. "It's okay. You're not trapped here."

Alexa backed away from him, not trusting the way her body reacted instantly to his proximity. "Who said I felt trapped?"

Drew rolled his eyes and spread his hands. "You're pacing. You've also refolded the same dish towel three times."

She glanced guiltily down at the dish towel in her hands and smiled as she set it down. "I guess I am feeling a little... restless. My usual routine has been thrown off, and I don't like sitting here waiting for my stalker to find me."

"That's understandable." Drew gave her a smile as he grabbed the orange juice from the fridge. He poured a glass and held the jug up, offering her a glass as well. When she nodded, he poured.

"So, let's get out. Where can we go that there won't be people who'll recognize you? And what would you like to do?"

Alexa shook her head. She sipped her orange juice, and after a few seconds of rolling back and forth on the balls of her feet, she let herself pace. Everywhere she could go in Willowdale, people would see her, recognize her. In a small town, where she'd lived for the better part of the last nine years, there weren't a lot of places she wasn't known.

"Want to help me work on my routine for the studio's open house?" Drew asked. "I know it's kind of aiding and abetting the enemy, but I do need to get some practice time in, and you and I are kind of attached at the hip."

Alexa turned away while she considered. Her thoughts from last night—that he was using her—seemed a bit maudlin in the morning light, and getting out of the house sounded tempting. Besides, if she worked with him on his routine, she would know what Crouching Tiger was up against, wouldn't she? Her lips quirked. "What kind of routine is it?"

Drew put a slice of bread in the toaster. "Nothing too showy, just a demonstration of basic fighting moves and how they would translate into self-defense." He cocked his head and grinned at her. "Think of it as an exposé of what works and what doesn't."

Oreo wandered in and nudged Alexa, so she dropped her hand to stroke the kitty's head. "Whatever you may think of us, Crouching Tiger teaches self-defense, too. We make all our students testing for a black belt prepare a self-defense routine. It's an opportunity for them to demonstrate that they've internalized fundamentals well enough to improvise." She looked back up at Drew. "So, yeah, I think I could help you. Maybe even teach you a thing or two."

Drew laughed. "Sounds good. I look forward to comparing notes." His toast popped up, and he flipped it out onto a plate then grabbed the butter. "There are painters at my place. The guy has a job during the week and mostly paints on the weekends. So, I can clear him out, or we can work out at Crouching Tiger. That is, if it'll be empty?"

Alexa topped off the cats' food bowl, since Fieldgar hadn't left much for the other two. She felt mixed emotions about Drew coming to her dojo, but she liked the idea of staying cooped up at the house with him all day even less. She tried to speak casually. "Crouching Tiger will be fine. We don't hold classes on Sundays and haven't scheduled a seminar for this week, or I'd be there." She paused to consider. "It's the most obvious connection to the stalker, though. What if he sees us going in and out or something?"

Drew nodded. "Good point. I'll text my painter, so we can use my place."

"Wait." Alexa held up her hand. She was suddenly loath to go to his MMA studio—partly because that would definitely be seen as aiding and abetting if it ever got out, but also for the purely irrational reason that she wanted to be somewhere that felt homey. "Do you really think Crouching Tiger isn't safe? I miss my house, even though yours is lovely, and I just... I'd rather be somewhere... familiar."

Drew considered that while he took a bite of toast and chewed. "There's no reason anyone would suspect you of being there, right? You don't usually go in on Sundays, even just to skip rope or something?"

"Never." Alexa shook her head. "Sundays, I'm usually home or running errands. Sometimes at the library."

"It should be all right, then," Drew said. "We'll slip in the back. We've got to go somewhere, or we risk having you take my house apart." He gave her one of those slow smiles, the kind that suggested intimate secrets.

Alexa headed back to the bedroom. "Let's go, then. I'll grab my gi." Getting out of the house was one thing they agreed on.

<hr />

Not an hour later, Alexa was beginning to doubt the nuances of their conversation over breakfast. She and Drew had been working on his routine, just as promised, but that wasn't all they were working on. If she didn't know any better, she would suspect Drew of designing his routine with the express end goal of intimacy. He seemed to be gearing every move to maximize physical contact. If he'd set out to seduce her through her favorite pastime, he couldn't have done a more effective job.

Of course, when was the last time she'd worked out with a fellow black belt? Not as another instructor, not even as a peer... but as someone she could get close to without embarrassment. Was she falling for Drew just because she'd shut all the other guys out?

"Now let's go for the throw," Drew said. She was tucked into him with her back to his chest, and his arms were wrapped around her in a spooning bear hug. "Make it look good—I want to impress the women in the crowd with the studio's practical skills."

Alexa shifted her hips so they tucked in close to Drew's groin, and dropped her center so she would have the heft she needed. Her whole body compressed, ready to pop up out of his grip and shift his upper body mass into the throw. "You want me to make it look good?" she asked. "Maybe you'd better work this move on them one-on-one. I suspect that's the most effective way to impress the chicks."

Drew laughed, the sound starting down in his chest, where Alexa could feel it building against her back, then bursting out. She took advantage of his momentary distraction to execute the move. *Pop, shift, dip the shoulder, and throw!* She flipped him harder than she meant to, but she took pity on him and used her grip on his right arm and shoulder to soften his landing.

But perhaps she should have thought through her "pity" and remembered whom she was dealing with.

Drew quickly turned the tables on her and used the momentum of his fall to pull her off-balance, tugging her down on top of him. Alexa landed half on and half off of Drew's torso, her chest thumping into his. But she wasn't crying uncle yet. She still had a hold of Drew's right arm, so she folded it back on itself to put him in an arm bar. She also raised her body up and shifted her weight so her knee could apply pressure to Drew's chest.

He gasped a chuckle but didn't tap out. His eyes found hers, and the seductive light inside them had gone from warm embers to a full blaze. "I could try a roll-out, but I think you've got me. The question is, what are you going to do with me?"

Alexa pulled back in confusion, and the tension went out of her arm bar. Drew quickly shifted his hips and flipped her over. It was a classic Brazilian jujitsu move and allowed him to roll free of her. But he didn't follow it up with any of the takedowns or holds she was sure he knew.

Instead, he let his arms hang loosely around Alexa, in what was almost a hug, and rested on his knees so he knelt in front of her. They were so close, it was hard to tell where his body left off and hers began. They were both breathless, and more than a little sweaty, but somehow

Alexa was sure the tiny tremor in her hand as she lifted it and set it on his chest wasn't fatigue. Had she put her hand there meaning to push him away or pull him close? She couldn't remember anymore.

It felt as though the moment they had shared the previous night in the library, when they'd almost kissed, was a small wave that had pulled back to sea, grown in power, and crested at this moment. The attraction between them was undeniable, and their differences suddenly seemed insignificant.

When Drew gently raised his hand to Alexa's face, she didn't pull away. He waited half a breath, just long enough to see she was with him on this, then leaned in to brush his lips across hers—a gentle caress full of tantalizing promise.

And suddenly, it was all too much—all the emotions, the self-control of staying okay as her life pinwheeled, the storming hormones she'd felt since coming to stay with Drew. In this moment, she didn't care about anything but riding the crest of this surge and enjoying it. Her hands came up and wrapped around Drew's neck, twining her fingers in his black curls. She pulled his mouth down to hers and hungrily nibbled at his lips.

Drew chuckled, a sexy rumble in his chest that made her teeth vibrate. He bent his head, and his tongue slid into her mouth, teasing her lips open and dancing with her own. Deepening the kiss, he shifted so Alexa was in his lap. She slipped into the mold of his body, and they fit together as though they'd never been apart. Drew's mouth on hers stirred up echoes of passion from years ago then took her to new heights.

When she pulled back to breathe, he nibbled at the corner of her mouth then trailed kisses along her cheekbone until he reached her ear. His teeth inched their way over the tender skin of her ear, and Alexa moaned. It felt so good, but he was moving too slow. She nuzzled her mouth against the curve of his neck and nipped him playfully. Squirming a bit to buy her hands some space, she tugged at the cloth V formed by his uniform top. She knew there were ties somewhere that would release his top, but her fumbling fingers couldn't seem to find them. Then Drew recaptured her mouth, and she forgot what she was trying to do.

Drew wrapped one hand around her backside, squeezing her bum, and Alexa arched up against his chest. Her mouth was too occupied to speak, but her body was begging him to go under her gi and touch her skin. Drew seemed to pick up on the signal and pulled her uniform up so his hands could trace up and down her back while their bodies rocked together.

The outer door of Crouching Tiger opened and banged shut with a clang that echoed around the dojo.

Alexa rolled away from Drew, and he was on his feet in one swift movement. Running in a half crouch so he stayed below the lobby windows, he positioned himself by the doorway between the lobby and the dojo.

Alexa jerked at her uniform, hurriedly trying to shove her top into place and get her belt positioned like it was supposed to be. Had the stalker found them? Should she hide? Should she get ready to fight?

Keri stepped into the open doorway.

"Drew, wait!" Alexa's cry was instinctive, but she realized immediately that she didn't have to worry. Drew knew better than to launch himself at an unidentified target.

He rose calmly from his crouch and nodded to Keri before turning away from her to tug his uniform into place.

Keri stepped forward uncertainly, her eyes taking in Alexa's tousled hair and hastily pulled-together uniform, then going to Drew, then back to Alexa. She grinned, and her eyes sparkled with laughter. "Should I even ask what's going on? I feel like the mom who just walked in on her teen and her teen's boyfriend."

"Very funny." Alexa accepted the hand Drew offered to help her up and tried to breathe through the hot flush that was setting her face on fire. "Master Hays requested that we promote good feeling between our schools, so Drew and I were working on the routine he's using for the opening ceremony of his studio." She yanked on her uniform again, watching Keri out of the corner of her eye. "We came here because there are painters at his studio."

Keri nodded sagely, but the glimmer didn't leave her eyes. "Uh-huh. Just working on the routine, helping each other out. So good of you." She stepped forward and gave Alexa's uniform a quick tug to settle it better into place then jabbed a finger at Drew's neck. "I know you always try to exceed Master Hays's expectations, but don't you think giving Drew a hickey was going above and beyond?"

Alexa's eyes darted up to Drew's neck, and sure enough, she'd given him a little red love mark. Worse, she could almost hear Keri's questions from the other day. She knew her friend would conclude from this that she was still as crazy about Drew as she'd ever been. Any minute, Keri was going to ask what they wanted for their wedding.

Ugh! With the way Drew had been acting plus her own crumbling resolve, that was the absolute last thing she needed. Why had she ever agreed to work out with him? "Okay, so maybe we got a little carried away." Her tone had more force than she'd intended. She sounded as though she was mad at Keri, but she couldn't seem to soften it. "It doesn't mean anything. You know how it is with army boys."

Drew stiffened beside her, and Alexa shifted. That might have come out a little more callous than she'd meant it. But in what way was it not true?

Keri shrugged and turned back toward the waiting room. "Whatever you've got going on, you need to decide now if you want it to be public. I came to open up for a birthday party. In five minutes, this place will be crawling with text-happy eleven-year-old girls, and your being here together will be spread all over Willowdale."

CHAPTER TWELVE

"**W**HAT?" ALEXA RUSHED TO THE doorway and looked out through the big lobby windows.

Out in the parking lot, a minivan had pulled up next to two cars, and girls were pouring out of the vehicles. A woman she recognized as Brianna's mom balanced an oversized cake and a box of party supplies. They all headed for Crouching Tiger's front door.

"Drew, you've got to get out of sight." Alexa shooed him toward the back door. "Wait at one of the shops down the street, please. I'll catch up to you as soon as I can."

Drew nodded, the motion a short jerk of the head. Alexa watched him go and couldn't help noticing how stiff his posture was. "I'm sorry for the wait," she called after him. "I should have checked the schedule—"

Drew lifted a hand to stop her protests and walked out the back door without looking back.

Alexa looked at Keri, who also seemed a bit stiff, then out at the crowd of girls approaching and shook her head. "I should have checked the schedule, but we haven't had a birthday party in so long, I just didn't think of it. And it seemed like a good idea to use Crouching Tiger, seemed like a good idea to get out of the house—"

"Sweetie." Keri put an arm around Alexa's shoulders and steered her toward the office. "I think you should wait in the office and let me get the party going. It's been a long couple of days. And while I'm sure Drew's been very hospitable, it's hard to not be in your own home."

"That's true," Alexa said. "I mean, his place is—" She stopped abruptly and looked at Keri in astonishment. "How did you know? We haven't told anyone…"

Keri laughed and nudged Alexa toward the open door to the office. "Don't worry. Your secret's safe with me. Wait in there, and we'll talk after I've got the party started."

Alexa nodded and had just shut the office door when she heard the ding of the chime out front and the sounds of girlish laughter fill the lobby. She smiled at the sound then went to the desk and sat down. As long as she was there, she might as well get some paperwork done and catch up on student accounts.

Her eyes fell on the orange candle with gold glitter that the stalker had left. The stupid thing was still waiting to be picked up by the police. They probably hadn't come to get it because it was the weekend. Plus, it didn't offer much in the way of evidence, and surely the police had more pressing emergencies than the attack on her cats.

Alexa turned the candle around so she could see her name written in wobbly capital letters. When she'd first found it sitting on her desk, she thought it the sweetest thing. Of course, she'd been sure it was from one of the five-year-olds in the Little Tiger class. She should have realized that none of them even knew her first name. She was Ms. Wolving to them.

It seemed kind of crazy to look back on the last two weeks and see how much her life had changed. There she was, hiding in the office until she could sneak out, so her sometime worst enemy and ex-boyfriend turned bodyguard could take her home and try to protect her from a psychotic stalker. Crazy didn't begin to cover it, especially when she seemed to have the self-control of a dragon in a gold mine when it came to Drew. What was wrong with her?

That was just it. She'd been running scared since the attack on her cats and had nearly run straight into Drew's bed. She snorted. That must have been what the term around-the-clock protection meant.

No way and no how was she going there. Going to bed with him would have been stupid and pathetic and would surely lead to heartbreak. Besides, hadn't she promised herself that she would watch him closely, so she would know if he was using her vulnerability to bring the schools together? How was she supposed to do that while she was throwing herself at him?

Alexa dropped her head into her hands and tried to scrub the fears and worries from her brain. What she really needed was to somehow regain a little control over her life and get her balance back. But she wasn't going to get that while she stayed with Drew.

Keri opened the office door and came in then closed it behind her.

Alexa dropped her hands from her face and looked up at her friend. "I'm sorry about how I acted back there. I guess I just… wanted to keep things under wraps, and I also felt embarrassed."

Keri shrugged and smiled. "It's okay. I think I pushed you a bit the other night at dinner. How are you holding up?"

Alexa shook her head. "I think that depends on your definition of holding up." They shared a smile, since that answer was an inside joke they referenced a lot. "I think it's time for me to find a new safe place to stay. Somewhere secure but by myself."

Keri looked her over carefully then swiveled the chair around in front of the desk so it was backward and sat down on it, facing Alexa. "Where did you have in mind?"

"Master Hays's townhouse," Alexa answered. "I have the keys back at my place. He gave me a spare set when they went out of town, so I could check on the plants if they were gone longer than expected. It's in a secure neighborhood that's gated. No one can get in unless they have the code or they're invited. And there's a cop who lives two doors down and could be there in minutes if I needed him."

"It sounds good," Keri said. "But are you sure? Shouldn't you check with—"

"I'm sure," Alexa interrupted. "Saving me from the bad guys isn't the only consideration here. We also have to consider my sanity, and for that, I need this move."

Keri nodded. "But speaking of bad guys, you still haven't filled me in on what's going on. I pieced some of it together when I ran into Dr. Springer at the street festival last night, and even more when I went by your place after it ended and found it empty. But this morning was the most revealing." She winked at Alexa. "Are you allowed to share details?"

Alexa gave a rueful laugh. "You know the juiciest stuff already." She glanced toward the door. It sounded as if the party was well under way. "Do you have to stay and babysit this? I could tell you everything on the way to my house if you like. After that, I'll need to run up to Drew's place and pick up my cats, but I can do that in my own car."

"No, I can leave," Keri said. "Brianna's mom hired two of the teenage black belts to help with the party. I'm just here to lock up when they're done, and that won't be for a while." She jumped up. "Let's go. I've been dying to hear the whole story."

Alexa laughed, the sound coming out a bit strangled. "Well, I don't know that it's worth dying for, but I'm sure it counts as crazy. Will that do?"

As Alexa came around the desk, Keri leaned in for a hug. "Better and better. You know I plan to take careful notes, right? When this is all finished, I want to send the script of your story into the daytime drama producers and see if I can make some cash out of it."

Alexa laughed again, this time for real. Her friend always knew how to cheer her up. "Fine by me. Just make sure you change my name and never credit the story back to me in any way. I've had my moment in the limelight, and I think I'll pass on another."

She followed Keri out the front door and over to her friend's car. As she walked, she glanced around for any sign of Drew but didn't see him. Which was perfect. If he knew what she was doing, he would surely try to stop her.

She waited until Keri had the car started then dialed the number for Drew's cell. When he answered, she went for a tone that was a cross between matter-of-fact and upbeat.

"Hey, it's Alexa," she said. "I've thought of somewhere out of your hair I can stay that's still safe. I'm with Keri now and will pick up my car from my house. Could I meet you at your place in, say, half an hour to pick up the cats?"

There was silence from Drew's end, and Alexa cringed. What must he think of her? Making a call like this after what had just gone down in the dojo would look as though she didn't trust him to stay out of her bed. And really, it wasn't her bed so much as her head and heart she was worried about.

"Does Detective Rawlings know where you're moving?" Drew asked. Alexa couldn't read anything from his voice.

"No, but I'll call her right after this. I'm sure she won't have a problem with the move. The place is—"

"Don't tell me," Drew said. "The fewer people who know, the better. I'll go pack your stuff and get the cats ready so you can make a quick retrieval. Drive safe."

He hung up.

Alexa looked at her cell. He hadn't argued or even sounded upset. On the other hand, that had sure been an awfully short conversation.

"He's on board?" Keri glanced at Alexa before turning her eyes back to the road. She made a right turn into Alexa's neighborhood.

"Yep. On board and packing my stuff for me," Alexa said. "Guess he was more anxious to get rid of me than I thought."

Keri snorted but didn't answer until she was parked in Alexa's driveway behind her little white car. "If you think that, you're an idiot. No guy is going to try and woo you back while you're in the act of rejecting him."

"I thought he'd be mad." Alexa got out of the car and surveyed her house. It looked fine—no broken windows and no signs of having been disturbed. Still, she felt no desire to go inside.

"Maybe he is. Drew doesn't strike me as the yelling type, though." Keri came around and stood next to Alexa. "Are we going in?"

She looked up and down the street. No sign of anyone, but she didn't know what she was looking for. Drew had asked her to call Detective Rawlings, and she planned to do that. But she wasn't sure she wanted to stand there until the detective sent an officer to check out her house, and she also wasn't sure she wanted to go inside without someone armed backing her up.

"You know what?" She wrapped her arms around herself. "Forget the house. Drew will pack the clothes I had at his place, and I'll manage fine with those. I'm pretty sure the keys to Master Hays's place are in the glove box of my car, 'cause I wanted them handy. So I don't need to go inside at all."

"Wow, Alexa." Keri put her arm around Alexa. "What happened here?"

Alexa shook her head, a frustrated roll from side to side. "The guy snuck into my house, probably using my own keys, and tried to drown my cats."

"What?" Keri cried. "When I talked to Dr. Springer at the festival, he said they'd been staying with him and were being watched, but that was all. Please tell me that you called the police."

"Yes, don't worry," Alexa raised her hands in mock surrender. "They've been involved since that night, and as soon as we're on the road again, I'll call Detective Rawlings and let her know about this change. Okay?"

"Okay, but I can't believe..." Keri stopped and took a slow, deep breath. "I guess I just hadn't realized it had escalated this fast. Do they have any leads?"

"A few, but not much." Alexa glanced up and down the street again. "Listen, I know this is crazy, and I wish I'd been able to tell you everything all along, but can the rest of the explanation wait?" She suppressed a shiver. "I really don't like standing here."

"Right, of course. But I'm going to stay right behind you. The birthday party will be going on for at least an hour, maybe two, so I have time."

Keri escorted Alexa to her car and stood watch while Alexa unlocked the door and checked to be sure Master Hays's keys were still in the glove box. Alexa would have found Keri's hovering amusing if she weren't so wired herself. When her fingers latched onto the small set of spare keys, she breathed a sigh of relief.

"You're okay following me out to Drew's place?" she asked Keri. "I may need backup if Drew tries to argue."

"Yeah, of course." Keri grinned. "Just don't take any of those little shortcuts you like without giving me lots of warning."

"Right, I'll stick to the main roads." Alexa jumped up and hugged her friend. "Thank you, Keri. I really appreciate it."

Keri hugged her back. "No problem. That's what friends are for, right?" She pulled back, and her smile was mischievous. "Tell you what, you can make me your maid of honor when you and Drew get hitched."

"Aagh, not even." Alexa groaned. "If that bridge ever existed, it's long since gone up in flames."

"All the same, my request stands." Keri grinned. "And make sure you pick a color I can wear, okay? No yellows. I look terrible in yellow."

Alexa just laughed and climbed into her car. Keri was impossible with her matchmaking. She started her car then waited while Keri backed out. As Alexa pulled out and pointed the car toward Drew's place, she shook her head and laughed ruefully. Maybe she hadn't argued with Keri more because it stung a little that Drew had let her go so easily. They were not a couple or anything of that sort, but they had developed some kind of bond over the last couple days, and she'd thought her safety meant more to him. But maybe he was wisely realizing that he needed space, too.

She waited until she was out of her neighborhood and had stopped for a red light before dialing Detective Rawlings's number. The light turned green, and Alexa slipped in her earpiece just as the detective picked up the phone.

"Hey, sorry to bother you." Alexa could hear a lot of background noise. "I hope this isn't a bad time."

"No, this is fine," Detective Rawlings answered. "What's going on?"

Alexa opened her mouth to speak, but from the corner of her eye, she caught sight of a big gray blur coming down the intersecting side street. A truck was going way too fast, and it headed straight toward her.

Alexa screamed. She swerved hard, hoping the driver had room to go around her. But instead of taking the space, the driver angled directly into her.

Alexa caught a glimpse of a face covered in a ski mask. Then the truck smashed into her car, and everything went dark.

CHAPTER THIRTEEN

DREW KNEW THAT HE'D BEEN short with Alexa, but he also knew he couldn't last much longer on the phone without reaching through it to shake her. So he'd hung up before he could try to break that particular law of physics.

He needed to clear his head and figure out what Alexa needed from him in order to be safe. First step, he needed to get back to the house.

He paid his bill at the coffee shop where he'd been waiting and headed for his truck. As he drove, he tried to figure out why Alexa had decided on this sudden shift to somewhere new. Was there any chance the stalker had threatened her? Or was she just reacting to their kissing and physical interaction? Emotions flashed through him as the memory of those kisses intruded, but he pushed them down.

The scene after Keri had shown up played through his mind. What was with Alexa's comment about "army boys"? He'd never been unfaithful to her back when they were dating, and he didn't know of any other army boy that was unfaithful. The comment had rubbed him the wrong way, that she would say something like that. Worse, it had him rethinking every angry remark she'd ever made about him and his MMA school. Was it possible Alexa was nothing more than a snob? Was she one of those anti-military types that thought the only difference between a soldier and a zombie grunt was the food they ate? He'd dealt with a lifetime's worth of that kind of crap from his father's family, even from Granddad for a time. The thought that Alexa might feel the same way made him sick.

He took a deep breath and shook his head to dislodge that train of thought. Focusing on the mission of keeping Alexa safe was what he needed to do. She didn't need a second stalker, so he would step back and leave her alone if that was what she insisted. But there was nothing wrong with doing what he could to persuade her to stay. His gut said her stalker wasn't going to back off, and Alexa on her own was inherently more vulnerable.

When he got to his house and walked in, he was immediately met by Ragbag and Oreo. The cats seemed happy to see him; Oreo started purring before he even petted her, and Ragbag found the laces on his shoes irresistible. It was nice, and not for the first time, Drew wondered if he should get a pet. He chuckled ruefully to himself. Maybe if he couldn't persuade Alexa to stay, he could still babysit her cats.

He spent a few minutes with the cats then went in search of Fieldgar, just to be sure the big orange tom was okay. Alexa would never forgive him if something happened to Fieldgar in his home.

He found Fieldgar sprawled on a pillow in the library, watching the birds flit around the feeder just outside the big glass doors. Drew bent down and stroked the cat's head then scratched around his ears. The pillow Fieldgar was lying on hadn't been on the floor when they'd left that morning, and Drew had to smile at the tom's ingenuity. It looked as though he'd first knocked it on the floor then dragged it in front of the window.

Drew continued to stroke the cat and look around the library. His mind went over the scene from last night. He and Alexa had come close to kissing, and he was sure she'd wanted to, but at the first tiny interruption, she'd run off to her room. Something was eating Alexa, something that was tied to her sudden decision to bail on him right after they'd gotten close at the dojo.

He racked his brain for anything he'd ever done that she might have taken as a sign he'd been cheating on her. But nothing came to mind. The summer they were together, he'd been totally wrapped up in Alexa and had no time or interest for anyone else aside from the obligatory time he'd spent with his granddad. The truth was he hadn't even dated much in the years since. It was true that army types—military guys— had something of a reputation, but he hadn't been one to take advantage of the serviceman mystique. Besides, he'd spent too much time in the field to dally even if he'd wanted to. If Alexa had him pegged as some kind of player, she had it all wrong.

Drew gave Fieldgar one last pat then went to gather Alexa's stuff. She would be showing up before long to collect her things, and he would ask her about what she'd meant by that comment. Carefully and gently because he didn't want to freak her out. But she could at least tell him to his face what he'd done to let her down.

His phone rang as he passed through the kitchen. Detective Rawlings's name showed up on the caller ID. He swiped the screen. "Drew Cosimo."

"Hey, what just happened?" Detective Rawlings asked. "Is Alexa okay?"

Alarm punched him in the gut. "I don't—"

"Are you with her?" the detective asked, as if Drew hadn't spoken. "She called to tell me something then screamed, and the call was cut off. What's going on?"

"She decided to move somewhere else." Drew noticed distantly that he was gripping the phone with white knuckles, but he couldn't make himself relax his grip. "She was with her friend, Keri. I'm back at my place. She asked me to pack up her stuff."

"Drew?" Detective Rawlings sounded distracted. "Hold on."

There was a pause in which Detective Rawlings talked to someone else. Drew tried to make out the conversation on the other end of the line without any success. Oreo brushed up against his legs and meowed. He reached down to pet her absently, still gripping the phone hard enough to leave ridges in his hand.

"I just got a report of an accident." Detective Rawlings was talking fast, and Drew heard doors opening and closing. "Alexa's car was hit by a truck, intentionally from the sound of it. She's en route to Blue State Hospital. She's in stable condition at the moment and asked for you before losing consciousness. You best get over there. I'll check in after I take a look at the site of the accident. And Drew? Don't leave her alone again."

She hung up, and Drew stood frozen for half a second, as if he'd taken the mother of all punches. Then the paralysis broke, and he was running for his truck before Oreo had even registered that he'd moved.

He slammed the door and revved up the engine, mapping out the fastest route to the hospital as the truck roared down the driveway.

Damn that girl, damn her beautiful hide. Detective Rawlings was right—he never should have let her out of his sight. He was letting his emotions cloud his judgment. He was losing sight of the mission. His mind sped a million miles a minute, watching for cars—or trucks—behaving oddly, maximizing his time as he sped across town, and planning for whatever scenario he was met with upon reaching the hospital. But underneath it all was one churning certainty—if this sicko had hurt Alexa in any lasting way, there would be hell to pay.

———————⊷⟨⟩⊶———————

Alexa woke up in a hospital bed, her hands taped up with IV needles. Her head felt as though someone had inflated a balloon inside her skull, blowing it up bigger and bigger until it had taken in more air than it could possibly hold. Then it popped.

A spot on the side of her head throbbed and stabbed painfully, but when she explored the area with her fingers, she couldn't feel anything but a cloth bandage. Slowly, as she sat quietly, a memory eased forward. She remembered a truck coming toward her and the horrible sense of an impending crash. Was Keri okay? She'd been right behind Alexa.

She heard a murmur of voices just outside her room. The door opened to admit a nurse, and behind her, Alexa caught a glimpse of Drew, leaning against the wall. She smiled, somehow feeling better just for having seen him.

"I like to see a smile. That's a good start." The nurse was on the shorter side, with dark hair and a pretty face. She spoke with a slight accent. She came over to check Alexa's monitors and prod gently at her scalp. "You're a very lucky woman, you know that? From what they told me of the accident, I'm surprised you came out of it without any broken bones or serious injuries."

"I'm glad to hear that. I guess what I feel is all my bones protesting the scare I gave them." Alexa held still so the woman could check her pupils. "How long was I unconscious?"

"You've been in and out for the last half hour, though I doubt you'll remember it. You were asking for that young man out there, and he's been very stubborn about staying close. Seems to think he's your bodyguard, but he acts more like a boyfriend."

Alexa smiled. "It's true, he is more like a bodyguard. These days bodyguards are the new boyfriends."

The nurse humphed at that, but she was smiling when she stood back. "All right, you're free to receive visitors. The doctor said he'll stop by and check on you again soon." She opened the door and motioned for Drew to come in.

Alexa met Drew's eyes as he sat down in the chair by her bed, and emotion washed over her at the concern on his face. "Hey." She tried to hit on a normal tone. "Is Keri okay?"

Drew smiled. "Yeah, Keri's a little rattled, but fine." Alexa attempted a tiny nod. I suppose my car is pretty crunched."

"I haven't seen it yet, but that's what they said." Drew was leaning back in the chair with his hands wrapped around each other in his lap as though he was afraid she would break if he touched her.

Alexa knew she was still fuzzy in the head and badly shaken. But she also knew that the only way she could deal with those things was if Drew helped her. She stretched her hand toward him.

He took it and stroked it gently with his thumb. "How are you feeling?"

"Pretty good, all things considered." Alexa touched the bandage on her head. "And pretty stupid. I shouldn't have bolted like that. I should have talked with you and considered my decision a little longer. Checked with Detective Rawlings."

Drew gave her hand a little squeeze. "I'm not sure that would have helped. He must have been watching your house, ready to ambush you along the route."

Alexa nodded, aware that he was going easy on her, and she was grateful for that kindness. "No, I was farther away than that. He must have been waiting for me. How did he know where I was going? Does he know me well enough to guess?"

"It's possible," Drew answered. "Master Hays's place was a logical choice. The same person who'd steal your keys when they were hanging in the office might also guess you would go to Master Hays's home. The students may have even known about your arrangement to water the plants."

Alexa shook her head. She'd been headed to Drew's house, not Master Hays's. But the pain from that quick headshake was enough to make her close her eyes and focus on breathing slowly.

Drew put his hand up to her cheek, soothing her pain with his touch.

Alexa smiled and turned her face into his palm. She opened her eyes to look up at him. "I'm sorry for what I said at Crouching Tiger about army guys. I was just… embarrassed, I guess, to be caught rolling around on the floor of my dojo."

Drew's eyes widened with a look she couldn't quite interpret. Then he smiled, and a radiant look of caring shone from his brown eyes. He leaned forward and touched his lips to her forehead in a feather-light kiss. "We'll talk about that later."

The door opened. Keri came in, followed by Detective Rawlings. They had almost identical expressions of fierce triumph, as if their team had just scored the first point in a tough sparring round.

"I believe we've figured out how the stalker knew where you were going," Detective Rawlings said. "I'm sending an officer to check it out right now."

Keri reached in to give Alexa a quick, careful hug. "It was the candle left in the office. There was a listening device of some kind attached to it, so the stalker could hear any conversations in there."

"That's still just a theory," Detective Rawlings said, raising a cautionary hand. "But it would explain both this ambush and the attack at the library. You talked in the office with me before the library attack, and in the office with Keri before this one. Neither time did you discuss your plans with anyone else, and neither did you know ahead of time you'd be going there. The stalker listening in on those conversations is the only way we can think of that he'd know where you were headed next."

Alexa turned to grab Keri's hands. "Did we talk about Drew while we were in there? Mention his name?"

"Yeah, I'm pretty sure we did," Keri said, her face reflective. "Just at the end."

"Great," Alexa said, making a face. "He knows about my safe haven." She slumped against her pillows. "That's just what we need."

"That's out now, anyway," Detective Rawlings said. "This hospital is full of people who saw Drew rush to your room. At least some of them will put two and two together, and word will get out. The two of you will just have to be extra watchful and use those safe rooms if it comes to that."

Drew nodded, looking warrior-like and determined.

Alexa squeezed his hand. All her objections to him as a person were starting to look kind of petty in light of recent events. All romance aside, she would rather have Drew at her back than a dozen ninjas.

She looked up at Detective Rawlings. "Do we have a name and a face for this guy yet? Can't you identify him from the car that hit me?"

"Unfortunately, no," Detective Rawlings said. "We can't even rule out Jason Stone since his parole officer has been slow getting back to me."

Alexa groaned. That was not what she was hoping to hear. "What do we know?"

The detective's face was sympathetic, but her tone was brisk. "The truck was a delivery vehicle that had been left with the keys in it while the driver stepped inside a store. We found it abandoned two blocks down from where you were hit. There were no witnesses as to who stole it. We'll check out the driver, but so far, his story seems to hold up."

"He came through a red light to hit me," Alexa said. "Is there a camera on that light? He was wearing a ski mask, but it would be better than nothing."

Detective Rawlings nodded. "It has one, and they're pulling a picture. We'll run it for any matches. Most of his face was covered, but you never know." She flipped open her notebook and pulled out a pen. "The better our timeline of events, the better our chance of catching him. So, let's discuss your version of today's events. What time did the two of you head to the dojo?"

Alexa answered the detective's questions as best she could, sometimes with help from Drew. It was difficult to keep her brain focused and responsive. Apparently, her mind thought staying conscious was overrated.

After Alexa had answered all the questions, Detective Rawlings flipped her notebook shut and stood. She walked the few steps to the window then back, appearing lost in thought. She stopped in front of the hospital bed and faced Alexa and Drew. "It appears today's accident was not premeditated because the perp acted on information as he received it. This attack also demonstrates escalating violence on the part of the stalker. After analyzing the scene at the library, we are reasonably sure the stalker did not intend the clay pot and books to make a direct hit. If someone had walked under the pot as it fell, they would most likely have been frightened, perhaps bruised or cut, but not killed." The detective paused to add weight to her words. "Today was different. The fact that you were not badly hurt was a happy accident. It appears that if the stalker can't gain control over you, he's willing to kill you."

CHAPTER FOURTEEN

ONCE AGAIN, ALEXA FELT THE gut-clenching fear she'd had when the truck swerved to hit her. If she closed her eyes, that moment replayed in her mind over and over like a pop-up window that refused to close.

She shook her head, which made her headache spike. In response to that pain, her body decided to jump on the bandwagon, reminding her that she had one hundred and three bruises she couldn't see. It was with an effort that Alexa managed to turn her brain back to the conversation.

Detective Rawlings was talking, her voice sober. "Your car is totaled, and even the delivery truck received considerable damage. We had hoped that a local hospital or urgent care center would get a visit from someone with a suspicious story around the same time, but so far, no one has shown up. It appears the stalker escaped without serious injury."

The detective took another stroll to the window and circled back. When she stopped in front of them, she rolled up on her toes, bouncing in a gentle swaying motion that was a sharp contrast to her concerned tone. "It is my opinion that the stalker concluded from what he overheard that you were staying with another man and attacked you out of jealousy. If that's the case, he will be more direct in going after you once he learns of Drew's visit here and"—her voice rose on a questioning note—"your going home with him?"

Alexa nodded, her face suddenly warm for no real reason. Drew's thumb moved in a circle on her skin. She had to pull her brain back from the physical touch between their hands and force her attention on Detective Rawlings. The edge of her focus was really frayed.

"What we really need is an ID, so that's where the majority of our focus will be," the detective said. "To that end, I've applied additional pressure on Jason Stone's parole officer, and I expect to hear back from him as to Mr. Stone's whereabouts within a day. We'll also work every other means available to us to try and identify this guy. In the meantime, your safety is our primary concern. I can have an officer swing by the house when he's free, but I lack the manpower to do more than that. Drew, we'll continue to count on you to protect Alexa."

"She'll be safe with me." The way Drew said it sounded as though he were etching the words into marble, where they would be preserved as a promise for generations. Alexa felt a glow of warmth.

The detective nodded and pulled out a file. She flipped through it then held it out to Drew and Alexa. "These are the notes on the case so far. Look them over and see if something connects. Our profiler is quite sure you know this guy, and you got a brief look at him today, albeit in a ski mask. Maybe inspiration will strike."

Alexa nodded soberly. What the detective didn't say, and didn't have to, was that identifying the guy might be their only chance of catching him before he managed to kill someone, and Alexa was at the top of the endangered list.

She shivered, suddenly exhausted, and was grateful when a rap at the door announced the doctor. He quickly cleared everyone out except for Drew, and after repeated reassurance that she would be carefully watched over the next twenty-four hours, he agreed to let her go home.

Keri came back in to help Alexa change, while Drew went out to wait in the hall.

"So," Keri began with a glance over her shoulder, "you still think that particular army boy is just good for a roll in the sack?"

Alexa laughed but didn't answer until they'd managed to get her shirt over her head without disturbing her bandage. "You know that's not what I think. Drew is a good man and has really gone the extra mile for me."

Keri raised her eyebrows in surprise.

Alexa smiled. "Okay, so now you know that's how I feel." Truth was, she hadn't known that herself two seconds ago.

"I'm glad you've come to that conclusion," Keri said. "He's been amazing. The second half every girl wishes she had at her back."

Alexa nodded. "It's true. It's just... I also know it's a long way from watching out for a girl in a crisis to a forever commitment with her when life gets dull again. I'm boxed in enough with everything that's going on—I don't need to corner myself any further."

Keri sighed and shook her head. "I hear you, girl. Trusting your heart is every bit as scary as risking bodily harm."

They were both quiet for a minute while Keri helped steady Alexa so she could slide into her jeans. "At the same time"—Keri put a hand on Alexa's arm and looked her soberly in the eye—"it's also true that the greatest payoffs in life take a willingness to risk ourselves. Even really happy relationships, like Master Hays and Joanne, started with one or both of them deciding that the other was worth the risk and making themselves vulnerable."

"I did that for Drew five years ago." The words popped out of Alexa's mouth. "He used my vulnerability to humiliate me and walk away."

"Yeah, but that was five years ago," Keri said. "Surely, you can see that he might have changed and grown, might be ready for this now."

Alexa shrugged, her eyes brimming with tears. Why she felt like crying, she couldn't say. Maybe it was general weepiness in the face of her aches and pains.

"Sorry, sweetie, I'm pushing again. Just think about it." Keri wrapped her arms around Alexa in a careful hug. "And try not to jump ship before you know for sure that the ship's going down."

"Like I did today." Alexa smiled. "All right, I won't jump ship. Not that Drew is likely to let me out of his sight."

"And thank goodness that's true," Keri said. "Are you sure you didn't pick him out years ago with this in mind? It seems a little fortuitous that your old flame happens to be a full-sized Special Ops action figure."

Alexa laughed again, despite the pain she felt with every chuckle. When they opened the door, Drew insisted that he be the one to wheel her out of the hospital in the obligatory wheelchair. She tried to submit graciously to his attention, even though there was nothing wrong with her legs.

She fidgeted and squirmed in the chair, insisting the nurse give her all instructions directly until she saw Keri and Drew exchange an amused eye roll. She paused, taking in the tight smile on the nurse's face. The woman took a deep breath and launched into another attempted explanation of Alexa's fuddled brain and what the schedule was for her pain meds.

"Never mind." Alexa passed the papers to Drew. "I trust you guys. I'll just do what you tell me to."

As soon as she said those words, she realized how rarely she let go and trusted anyone. The words almost felt as though they were straight out of someone else's vocabulary. She knew what they meant in theory, but she had no personal connection to them.

She was quiet as Drew drove her to the pharmacy to pick up her prescription painkillers. Drew insisted that she take the first dose immediately before they headed back to his house. Of course, she nearly fell asleep sitting up on the ride home.

Before she knew what was happening, Drew came around to her side of the truck and lifted her out. For half a second, her old walls slammed up, but just as quickly, they crumbled again. She snugged her arms around his neck and relaxed into him. She closed her eyes for the short walk into the house and kept them closed as they crossed into the brightly lit rooms. She heard the cats meow. Drew's voice rumbled in his chest as he asked her something. Her reply was nothing more than a mumble.

Then she was tucked between smooth sheets, and a comforter was pulled up over her body. Drew shifted away from her, and she reached out for him. He tucked Fieldgar into her arms and promised to be right back. After one deep blink of her eyes, he was by her side again, and she gave up her struggle to stay awake.

Drew stretched out on top of the covers, his body running alongside Alexa's. He smoothed the blanket a little higher, and she snuggled into it. Her face was mobile in her sleep, alternating from blissful contentment to pain and worry. When the pain lines creased her forehead, Drew smoothed them out.

When he touched her, she sighed in her sleep and seemed to rest better, so he continued to run his fingers over the bones of her face.

She was so beautiful. Perhaps what he felt now was painting his previous memories, but it seemed as though he'd loved her face forever. In all these years, she'd remained in his mind as the girl he was growing toward and coming back to.

He'd been a fool to walk away from her five years ago, more so given how he'd done it. He had regretted his harsh words as soon as he'd said them, but he'd been too stiff with pride to unsay them and too afraid of needing her to reach out. But that was five years ago, and thankfully, he'd learned a thing or two since then. What he wasn't sure of was whether Alexa would ever give him another chance. She'd apologized for her comment about army boys, but he would be willing to bet she never would have come back if it hadn't been for her accident.

She stirred in her sleep, and her hair fell across her face. He brushed it back, careful to smooth it away from the bandage on her temple. Her hair slipped through his fingers like silk… or feathers. Drew grinned at that last thought.

When he was a boy, he'd stayed for a summer with his mother's parents on their farm in Pennsylvania. They'd had a whole flock of reddish-gold and brown chickens, and he used to chase them all over the pasture, trying to catch one. Eventually, he got tired of running and started making whistles from the tall grass. That led to braiding the grass into ropes, and somewhere in the middle of that project, he kept having to shoo one particular chicken away. She took to hanging around him, and eventually, he could turn and catch her without getting up off the ground. When he did, he would snug her close and stroke the hen's smooth, soft feathers. She didn't seem to mind too much. She had never pecked him and was slow to move away once he'd set her down.

Stroking Alexa's hair, Drew smiled to himself. Maybe that was what he needed to do now. Just swallow his pride and stick around, even when she acted stiff. Eventually, if he just kept things pleasant, she would stop running and accept him. Or so he hoped. Meanwhile, he would keep her safe from her stalker if it was the last thing he did.

He tucked the blanket around her a little more snugly and made sure Fieldgar was handy if she needed something to hug. Time to do a check of the house.

As he rolled away from Alexa, a flurry of yellow and orange leaves blew by, smattering against the window. In the darkening sky, they stood out like bright flecks of flame. He'd heard earlier that a storm was coming. Lots of rain was predicted, as well as high winds. Typical for this time of year, but terrible timing for Alexa and him. Nothing like the sound of a storm to cover the approach of a would-be intruder.

Starting with the master bathroom and working his way around the upstairs, he checked each window. Once he was convinced everything was secure upstairs, he stepped back into his bedroom to check on Alexa.

She stirred in her sleep. Her body stretched out under the covers, accentuating her womanly shape, and Drew felt a stirring of interest in his lower parts. He took a firm rein on his desire and tucked the blanket back around her feet. She looked so sweet, snuggled under the covers. A stranger would never guess the resilient, fighting spirit inside nor fully understand her keen mind. She really was amazing.

He waited until Alexa was back to a deep sleep then headed downstairs. He would finish the perimeter check then whip up a snack. It was almost time to wake her up so he could check for a concussion, and he wanted to get a little food into her while she was awake. Soup wouldn't take long to make.

As he started pulling out cans of beans and chicken broth, Drew decided to turn on a nightlight in the guest bedroom and perhaps set something up in the bed. If he stacked pillows under blankets, they could be mistaken for someone asleep. His gut said the stalker was on the move somewhere in the town tonight, and over the years, Drew had learned to trust his gut.

CHAPTER FIFTEEN

ALEXA WOKE WITH A SENSE of loss, and for a minute, she couldn't place where she was. Then she noticed Drew's jacket thrown over the back of a chair and one of his martial arts books on the bedside table. She was in his room, and now that she thought about it, she vaguely remembered him asking her if it was okay to put her there. He'd said something about wanting to protect her. At the time, his question had seemed inordinately silly, but that must have been the pain meds talking.

Fieldgar jumped off the chair where he'd been curled up and cat-footed across the puffy duvet to poke his nose under Alexa's fingers. She stroked his head then cupped his face in her hands and gave him a kiss on the nose. He hated that, but she couldn't help herself.

She heard Drew's voice on the stairs and looked up to see him come through the doorway with a tray in his hands and the other cats trailing him. The scent of delicious chicken broth preceded him into the room.

He looked slightly harassed, but he smiled when he saw her. "I gave them a little of the chicken I put in the soup, and now they won't stop following me and begging for more. I keep telling them it's been soaked in salsa and they don't want it, but they're quite sure I'm holding out on them."

Alexa laughed. "It's probably true that Ragbag doesn't really want it, but Oreo has rather gourmet tastes. She'd probably love it and forever after beg for salsa to go with her chicken. And be warned, she always gets her way in the end."

Drew came across the room and set the tray on the bed, across Alexa's lap. "I stand forewarned. Let's hope none of the soup spills where she can get it."

On the tray was a knotted wood bowl, filled with little round slices of toasted Italian bread. Alongside it was a deep dish filled with a clear soup that was chock-full of beans, chicken, and salsa. Drew had also peeled and separated an orange, which was on a plate next to the glass of water.

"This looks fantastic." Alexa scooped up a bite of bread and tried the soup. "And tastes even better. Thank you."

"The doctor said to wake you every hour or so for the first half of the night, and to make sure you eat when you take your pills." Drew slid the chair with his jacket closer and pulled a pill bottle out before sitting down.

When Alexa took the pill from his hand, their fingers brushed. The little tingle that followed warmed her faster than the soup. She smiled at Drew, and he smiled back, but then he stole a piece of bread and sat back, out of her reach.

They ate in silence for a few minutes. Alexa enjoyed the feeling of being warm, safe, and reasonably pain free. Drew's company didn't hurt, either.

Oreo jumped up on the bed and nosed through Alexa's tray, looking for any likely bits. When Alexa slipped a bit of chicken off her spoon so the cat could have it, Fieldgar prowled over to get a taste too.

"Feeding them off your spoon, eh?" Drew asked with a chuckle. "No wonder they seem to think they're entitled."

Alexa struck a snotty pose. "For your information, cats always feel entitled, and there isn't a single thing you can do about it."

"Okay, okay." Drew threw his hands up in mock surrender. "I don't have a problem with that. Around my sister's kids, I prefer the status of indulgent uncle, anyway. There will be time enough to figure out the discipline half of things when I have kids of my own."

He leaned back in the chair, and when he spoke, his voice was musing. "I've always thought how great it would be to have a child of my own and guide them in their search for life's answers. I think most kids feel they're missing something. Being a parent ought to be a chance to explore along with them, help them identify what it is they're seeking."

Alexa stared at Drew, the spoon forgotten in her hand. "You want to be a dad?"

Drew shrugged. "Of course. Why wouldn't I?"

"Because..." Alexa fumbled around in her brain. "Well, because you never seemed the type to—" She cut herself off. She'd almost said that he didn't seem the type to stick around once the baby showed up.

Drew frowned. "My dad was gone a lot, and my mom left when I was ten. So yeah, maybe I don't have lots of firsthand memories of good parenting to draw on. But that's all the more reason I want to be a good dad someday when I get the chance."

Alexa was struck speechless—first, because she was hit by how wrong most of her perceptions about Drew had been. And second, because she could so easily see what a great dad he would make.

Drew seemed to realize they'd drifted into uncharted conversation waters. He shifted and spoke casually into the silence. "I suppose taking care of your cats is like being a mom for you."

Alexa's melting heart felt a quiver go through it, not entirely unpleasant, but still... unsettling. All her friends knew how much she hoped to someday have a family of her own, but she wasn't sure she was ready to chat with Drew about parenting. It felt incredibly intimate, even more so than kissing in some ways.

She put on a grin and spoke lightly. "Maybe. I guess it will depend on how much like a cat my someday-kids are. I suspect they'll need a bit more than food, water, some cuddles, and safe places to climb."

Drew laughed, but she was grateful he also let the subject drop. He leaned down to pick up Ragbag. "What about this guy? How come he doesn't get a share of the helpings?"

Alexa swallowed a mouthful of Italian bread and shrugged. "He doesn't want it. He'd rather explore and get into trouble, take the house apart or escape out the door when you least expect it."

"A cat after my own stripe, then." Drew's eyes were distant as his hand stroked Ragbag's fur. "I never understood the other kids. Wasn't looking for the same things they were. Maybe because I moved around so much and came to like the constant change. Or maybe I just wanted adventure."

Alexa swallowed around the lump that seemed to be blocking her throat. Drew's eyes were moody and open, giving her a look deep inside the man that had claimed the right to protect her. "And did you find adventure?" Her voice sounded just a little funny in her ears. "Did you find what you were looking for?"

Drew's hand stilled on the cat, and his eyes suddenly came back—deep brown and intensely focused on hers. "Yeah, I think I have."

Alexa wanted to say something light, flippant, and change the mood. Instead, a sudden flash of unbidden images filled her mind. She remembered the first night she'd had sex with Drew, five years ago. They'd spent a lot of time rolling around while making love, but for the act itself, he'd been on top, his eyes looking straight into hers with such intensity and tenderness, she almost couldn't breathe. The intimacy of that moment was almost shocking, like jumping feet first into cold water. But the pleasure that went with it was beyond anything she'd ever imagined.

Fieldgar bumped Alexa's hand, looking for more chicken, and she dropped her eyes. Her face felt heated, and her throat dry. She grabbed the glass of water and used the pretense of taking her pills to gulp down half the glass.

This conversation and all the revelations she'd uncovered about Drew in the last couple days were enough to make her head spin, even without the excuse of having been recently whacked in a car accident. She looked away from Drew, down at the blanket, then around the room.

"I need… I need a few minutes," Alexa said. "To use the bathroom and get ready for bed. Those pills are going to make me sleepy again, right?"

"Quite likely." Drew got to his feet. "I left your pajamas folded in the bathroom, right through there." He pointed to a door adjacent to the vanity and sinks. "Just let me know if you need anything. I'll be close by while you're sleeping, and I'll need to wake you up again in an hour or two."

Alexa nodded. Her fingers plucked at the loose threads in the duvet as she watched Drew walk to the doorway. When he'd almost closed the door behind himself, she spoke up. "Drew?"

He poked his head back in.

"My sleeping in your bed… I can't remember what you asked me. This is just for protection reasons, right? 'Cause this room is more secure?"

Drew grinned, and for a moment, his face looked positively devilish. "Don't worry, I'm not going to ravish you in your sleep. I'll only be in here when you need me."

"Oh. Good." Alexa nodded, a little annoyed with herself at the spark of arousal she felt when he grinned like that, and even more annoyed that she was maybe just a teensy bit disappointed.

"Good night, Alexa," Drew said. "Sleep well." He closed the door.

Alexa climbed gingerly out of the bed and made her way to the bathroom. She cringed when she saw the bruising on the side of her face that had hit the window. She looked awful. But whether she cared about that because she was naturally vain or because she planned to seduce Drew sometime tonight, she really couldn't have said. That uncertainty seemed kind of symbolic of her general state of mind right now.

She'd gone from being a regular small-town librarian to someone who had a stalker among her friends, whom she was hiding from in the bed of a Ranger bodyguard. And on top of that, she suspected she was falling in love with her ex, who also happened to be her direct competitor. It was all just a bit much. So many of her beliefs had been toppled lately, and so much of her world had turned upside down. It was as if she'd gone for a sunny cruise but instead found herself tossing about on stormy seas. It was going to take her a bit to get her land legs back. The question was, what did she want her life to look like when she did get back on her feet? To that question, she had no answer.

CHAPTER SIXTEEN

COLD FEAR WASHED OVER DREW, clenching his gut and pinning his body to the chair he'd pulled close to the bed, where he sat watching over Alexa. The blue light from the laptop cast eerie shadows, reaching out long chilly fingers toward Alexa's sleeping face. He stared at the masked face looking back at him from his laptop screen. Those eyes… they sparked a roil of dread and recognition.

After leaving the hospital, Detective Rawlings had emailed him the blurry red-light photo taken moments before the truck smashed into Alexa's car. The bottom half of the face in the photo was obscured by a ski mask, but the area around the eyes was open, and Drew was accustomed to identifying teammates and targets from half-hidden faces. More importantly, he recognized the expression of intense cruelty in those eyes, the need for domination that twisted the attacker's features. He'd seen those eyes with that expression before.

Taking control of the adrenaline rushing through him, Drew opened a second window on his laptop to Crouching Tiger's website so he could double-check his suspicion. Detective Rawlings had suspected the stalker was someone connected to the school, but Drew had seen all the students who interacted regularly with Alexa, and nothing before had sparked recognition. He clicked through the Crouching Tiger website and found the pictures showing recent tests, including students who'd tested.

Stuart Odel tossed a mocking smile off the page. Stuart was a brown belt, according to the Crouching Tiger website. And based on the date of his last testing, he was overdue to test for black. Drew couldn't believe he hadn't made the connection before, but Stuart's new look was as good as any disguise. The brown belt had recently transformed himself from an average-looking guy to a wannabe Tibetan monk, complete with a shaven head and long dangling mustache. He also could have passed for a South Seas pirate. Either way, he wasn't pulling it off. The website had pictures from both before and after Stuart's transformation, so putting them together was easy.

Drew leaned back and scrubbed his hand over his face. His eyes rested on Alexa, still peacefully sleeping. He realized that he'd seen Stuart several times since this whole thing began—at the dojo on the day of the break-in and standing in line to buy a used book at the library on the day Alexa was nearly hit. Drew hadn't recognized him because the new look changed Stuart's face. He'd also lost weight in the years since Drew had last seen him. Still, Drew was surprised he hadn't made the connection, and even more surprised Stuart didn't have a rap sheet that would have flagged Detective Rawlings's attention.

Drew had known Stuart as a kid. Stuart's dad had been the head custodian at the same college where Drew's granddad was the dean. Every once in a while, Drew and Stuart would be tossed together at a college Christmas party. Drew hadn't liked him then. He was the kind of kid who let others take the blame for his pranks. But it was near the end of the three-week leave when Drew and Alexa were dating that he'd gotten to know Stuart better than he ever wanted to.

It had been a lovely evening, and Drew was walking back to his car after dropping Alexa off at her friend's house, where she was spending the night. He had just gotten his orders and knew his leave was up, but that evening, Alexa had been his whole focus. The moon shone as bright as a giant spotlight in the sky, and a spat of rain earlier in the evening had cleared the air.

Just before he reached his car, Drew heard a girl sobbing. He stopped to listen and turned back toward the noise. When he reached the cluster of trees where the girl was crying, he saw a figure standing over her and heard a male voice speaking in low, ugly tones—Stuart's voice. When the girl didn't stop crying, Stuart drew back his foot and kicked her in the stomach.

Drew leapt forward and tackled Stuart. The fight would have been over pretty quickly, except the girl started screeching and kept getting in the way, trying to separate them. Then there was the sound of police sirens, and before Drew knew it, he and Stuart were sitting in the back of a police car, on their way to be questioned. Apparently, the girl had been gang raped earlier in the evening but had run from the scene when the cops arrived—possibly because she'd been there to buy a joint. When the officers found her with Drew and Stuart, they thought they'd caught the perpetrators.

Waiting at the police station for the next hour had to have been the lowest point of Drew's life. He was terrified that his granddad would hear, or that by some miscarriage of justice, he would be found guilty and court-martialed, never able to accept his first mission as a Ranger. But perhaps the worst part of it was that he had to spend the hour with Stuart, who laughed at the whole situation. He said he knew the girl would set them free because she was his girlfriend and he was the only man who would take her now. He also didn't see why she was upset about the rape because she'd offered her body to men in return for drugs or cash in the past—he'd even arranged it for her once or twice. So what if she got a bit more than she bargained for this time? What was the big deal?

It turned out that Stuart was right on one count—the girl did clear them of being suspects. Neither of them was even booked. The fact that Drew had a stamped ticket from the dinner theater he and Alexa had attended—and that the show was an hour's drive away—probably helped. Drew didn't even need to call Alexa to confirm that he'd been with her.

But when he and Stuart had walked out of the police station, he'd barely been able to hold back from punching Stuart when the jerk walked up to his girlfriend and kissed her roughly. Her lips were swollen from her ordeal, and she was obviously still in a state of shock, but that didn't seem to matter to Stuart. He just grabbed her by the hand and started dragging her off to a party.

Drew stepped in and offered the girl a ride home. It seemed like the least he could do. But that frightened her, and she pulled back, shaking her head and crying. Stuart grinned in triumph and reached for the girl again, but she started screaming and shoved him away then ran off. Stuart would have gone after her, but Drew stepped in his path.

They were standing just outside the police station, so although Stuart looked mad enough to kill, nothing came of it. Still, Drew never forgot the murderous look in Stuart's eyes. His girlfriend had been gang raped, and he didn't see the problem. But Drew had witnessed her humiliate Stuart, and he knew that would never be forgiven. Stuart told Drew he would be watching for a chance to "give Drew a taste of his own medicine," whatever that was supposed to mean.

As for Drew, he was moody and preoccupied when Alexa called later, and he was rude when she asked about his night, cutting her off. He was such a twit. He didn't even tell her a proper good-bye. But at the time, he had just shut down and closed her out. The next morning, he'd shipped out for his first mission, and he'd thrown himself into the work, completely blocking out all memory of the disastrous end to his leave.

Now that creep Stuart was stalking Alexa, and he must know that she was in Drew's protection. As if it weren't bad enough that he was dangerously obsessed with Alexa, what would he do once he knew he could get back at Drew through her?

Setting his laptop aside, Drew rose and walked quietly to the bedroom door and out into the hall. Swinging the door almost shut behind him, he pulled out his cell phone and dialed the number for Detective Rawlings. As he waited for her to pick up, he couldn't help pacing in the hall beside the stairs, but he tried to do it quietly. No need to wake Alexa if he didn't have to. Hopefully, Detective Rawlings could send some officers to pick up Stuart Odel, and this would all be over by morning.

"Hey, Drew, what's up?" Detective Rawlings didn't sound sleepy, so she must have been on duty.

Drew stopped at the end of the hall, where he could look across a spare room to a dark window. "I think I've ID'd our guy. Name is Stuart Odel. He's a brown belt at Crouching Tiger and a local to Willowdale. He recently changed his hair in a big way, but I made the connection when I saw the photo."

"Those photos don't show much of his face. How sure are you?" Detective Rawlings asked. "Besides, he was on the list of men Alexa had dated, so we checked him out. He came up clean."

"I recognize his eyes. I have reason to remember them. Just dig deeper, would you?" Drew walked across the spare room to look out the window but couldn't see anything. The night was too dark. Not a star was shining. "I have a hard time believing he's kept his hands completely clean. And I think he was trained as a locksmith. He has an uncle in the business who used to help his dad on campus."

"All right," Detective Rawlings said. "You sound sure. Jason Stone's parole officer finally got back to me. Jason is sitting quiet, just where he's supposed to be, and hasn't met anyone suspicious or made any phone calls that might have allowed him to arrange this. So that lead is dead, anyway. We'll see what we can find out about Stuart. With one guy to focus on, we can put a little more into the search and hopefully turn something up."

"Thanks, I appreciate it." Drew hung up and walked back into the bedroom.

Alexa was sitting up in the bed, looking more alert than she had the last few times Drew had woken her. The clock on the table beside her read five thirty a.m., so it was later than Drew had realized.

"I heard voices," Alexa said.

He nodded and sat in the chair beside the bed. "I called Detective Rawlings." He hesitated, unsure exactly how to go on. "How well do you know Stuart Odel?"

"Not really well." Alexa's eyes roamed around the room, making her seem restless. "He's pretty good in point sparring but has a hard time taking correction. He and Master Hays had a falling out about a month ago, but he seems to have gotten over it. Why?"

When Drew didn't immediately answer, her eyes came back to his face, and she gasped. "Are you serious? You think Stuart is my stalker?"

Drew nodded. "He's changed his hair recently and added that mustache, but when I saw him in the ski-mask photo, he looked familiar. I'm sure."

Alexa shook her head, but more in puzzlement than denial. "We had a soft date set up, but I had to cancel it. I didn't think he liked me that much or cared that we didn't go out. He could be funny sometimes, but I didn't really like him. Why would he do this?"

Drew shook his head. "Who knows? Maybe he thought you insulted him by cutting off your date this summer. You canceled at the last minute?"

"Yeah, but that was as much him as me," Alexa said. "Ragbag was just a little thing then and had come down with a cough. I took her to the vet, but things ran late, so I called Stuart and told him we'd have to go to a later movie if he still wanted to do that, and when he pressed for a time, I told him I didn't know how soon I'd be ready. He seemed a little annoyed and said to forget it, that we'd just try again another time."

"Did he ever ask you out again?" Drew asked.

Alexa shook her head, then her eyes flew wide. "Yes, he did, but I'd forgotten. It didn't seem like a date, you know. He just asked me if we could get coffee after sparring one day, but I was attending a book festival with Keri and Brian, so we let him tag along. And honestly, I didn't pay him much attention. You think he did all this because of that?"

Drew shrugged. "Maybe. A stalker's reasons wouldn't make sense to us, 'cause what drives him is sick and obsessive, by definition. But I'm pretty sure it was him. You remember the day at the library, when the pot fell? I saw him buying a used book from the sale table. If he paid cash, there wouldn't be any paper trail placing him on-site. He's clever, I'll give him that. Who knows how many other times he's been near you at the time of an attack?"

Alexa nodded, her face troubled. "The day you helped me with my tire, he pulled up and offered to help. At the time, I didn't think about it, but now it seems odd he didn't stick around once he saw you."

"You're probably lucky he didn't realize then that we were together," Drew said. "He doesn't like me. We had a run-in several years ago. Things might get a lot worse now that he knows you're with me." As soon as the words "you're with me" were out of his mouth, he realized that might not have been the best way to put it.

Alexa said nothing but simply raised her eyebrows in a questioning look.

"With me, as in, you're under my protection," Drew clarified. He didn't want to presume anything and scare her off by his presumption.

Alexa's eyes narrowed. "What are you not telling me? Why would my being near you be any worse than my being close to anyone else in Stuart's book?"

Drew rose and paced the floor. It was time he came clean with Alexa about that night. Given how Stuart was behaving, he couldn't rule out that the sicko's original interest in her was piqued as a result of her and Drew's history. "I know you've been angry with me about how we parted." He glanced at Alexa and saw surprise mixed with... pain? Distrust? He had to look away. "I was involved in an incident with Stuart and his then-girlfriend, just at the end of my leave."

Alexa sat quietly on the bed, listening, while Drew roamed around the room and told her about that night. If he thought thinking about it had been embarrassing, relating it all—out loud—to Alexa was much worse. He could see what an idiot he'd been. He should have tried harder to get help for Stuart's girlfriend. He should have better understood the dynamics of what he was dealing with. And he definitely shouldn't have been cold and rude to Alexa when she called later that night just because he was a mess inside.

He stood at one of the windows, looking down at the yard, as he finished up the sordid tale. He paused before continuing. The next bit was even more difficult, and it came out in a low voice. "I'm sorry I lacked the maturity to tell you what was going on. I think my coping tools at the time were to push something aside if it was pushable or, lacking that, bottle it up. But that's no excuse, and I know I acted like a jerk."

He waited for Alexa to say something, but there was only silence. He turned just in time to have her slip into his arms.

"I think that is the sweetest story I've ever heard." Her face was turned up to him, and her arms went up around his neck. It felt so right, but the back of his brain wondered if she should be doing this. What about her pain? He tried to mentally calculate when Alexa's last pain meds had hit her system, and he was pretty sure she wasn't due any.

Then her mouth was on his, and Drew's thoughts scattered as she kissed him with a passion that washed away every memory of any other kiss. Her full lips pressed against his, and their tongues twined. The heady taste of her scent filled his senses and rolled across him like a fine wine.

Molding her body to his, Alexa wrapped one leg around him. Given that she apparently only slept in the top half of her pajamas, her legs and sexy tush were right on level with his hands and felt like heaven in a woman-shaped bottle.

With their mouths still locked together, Drew picked her up and settled her hips against his own. His hands cupped her buttocks, kneading her, and their pelvic areas ground together in a dance of their own.

Alexa arched her back, pressing her breasts into his chest. It felt so good to hold her, savor her. Years of pent-up need surged through him, threatening to overwhelm the shreds of control he retained.

He moved his mouth down her throat, his kisses hungry. Alexa gasped and tipped her head back. His lips devoured the newly exposed skin she offered him, but it wasn't enough. He wanted more. He pulled back for a second, intending to undo a few more of those buttons, but the look on Alexa's face arrested him.

Her beautiful face was flushed with desire, a girlish pink on her cheeks. Her eyes were closed, and her mouth was open just a breath. The effect was lovely and seductive, but there was something else— something terribly sad, almost heartbreaking, in the determination of her passion and the closed lids behind which she hid her eyes.

Drew blinked, trying to clear his brain. His fingers slid up from her bottom to wrap around her waist. His thoughts were sex-blurred, but he knew there was something he wasn't getting. Something was off about this. Why had Alexa come onto him so strongly? Why now?

Softly, ever so softly, he drew Alexa back to him and kissed her gently on the mouth. She opened her beautiful hazel eyes wide, staring straight into his. She looked so vulnerable, so afraid.

Drew eased her down until her feet were back on the floor. He didn't want to make love to her because she was frightened. He wanted her to be swept away by more than passion. Real and abiding love was what he wanted—love that they would build on until it would last forever. This wasn't going to be just another tumble in the sack.

His voice was husky when he spoke and rougher than he intended. "This isn't the time, Alexa."

Confusion and embarrassment flashed across her face, followed quickly by anger. She pushed away from him, stumbling a little in her haste. Her fingers went to the neck of her pajama top, pulling it closed. She looked like a startled rabbit, ready to run.

"Alexa." Drew reached out and captured her wrist with his hand. "Stop. There's nothing to—"

She twisted her arm up then flung her hand down across his fingers, breaking his grip. She snatched Fieldgar from his snoozing spot on the bed and rushed out of the room. As she passed the door, she hooked it with her foot and slammed it shut behind her.

CHAPTER SEVENTEEN

WHEN THE DOOR BANGED SHUT behind her, Fieldgar started in Alexa's arms then twisted to get down. At first, Alexa clung tighter, not wanting to be rejected by him, too, but when she faced the stairs and realized how off her balance was, she let him go. The last thing she needed was to take a tumble down the stairs while carrying her cat.

Okay, so maybe that wasn't the last thing she needed. Several worse scenarios came to mind pretty easily, and half of them mimicked the scene that had just played out in Drew's bedroom. The other half involved her stalker. Life was full of fun options.

She probably shouldn't have run. But how could she have stayed? She'd literally thrown herself at him, and he'd put on the brakes just when things were getting going… just like last time.

Ugh. Stalker or no stalker, this was something she couldn't work out on her own.

Alexa started down the stairs with a hand on the rail. It was her subconscious's fault. She'd woken from one of her steamy dreams, filled with Drew and images of them twined together. Then he'd identified Stuart as her stalker, which was a shock but also a relief. Especially given that they no longer suspected Jason Stone. Stuart didn't scare her much, not like Jason had. She just couldn't take him seriously. Now that Detective Rawlings had a name and a face, it wouldn't take her long to catch him. And besides, it was such a relief to finally know who was after her. She'd hated the feeling of a shadowy figure prowling in the background, watching for a vulnerable moment. It had felt as though she were fighting an invisible opponent.

What really undid her was Drew coming clean about why he'd dropped her five years ago and what a gentleman he'd been even then to that poor girl. All Alexa's reservations about him hadn't been enough to keep the surge of hormones in check. She was just so tired of wanting him, needing him, and not having him. She needed relief from the pressure and thought he would welcome it too. Instead, he'd waited until she was fully committed and had really thrown herself at him then slapped her offer right back in her face.

She was just—beyond confused, her mind not so much going in circles as it was ping-ponging off the insides of her skull.

She reached the guest bedroom and locked the door behind her. Then she went straight to the bed and climbed beneath the covers. She snuggled down in the deep down comforter and swiped her cell screen to call Keri.

"Hello—Alexa? Are you okay?" Keri's voice was sleepy and concerned.

Alexa winced. She'd somehow forgotten it was the middle of the night. "Yeah, I'm fine! I'm so sorry to wake you. I just wanted to talk."

"Babe, you are always welcome to call." Keri laughed a little, sounding more awake. "What's up?"

Alexa paused for half a breath then took the plunge. "I think I'm in love with Drew."

"Well, of course you are," Keri said. "He's hunky, a great cook, a devoted protector, and good to you. But what made you realize it?"

Alexa had to laugh at Keri's total lack of reaction to her big news, and she found herself spilling everything. She told Keri about the stalker's suspected identity, Drew's confession about what had happened before, and then an abbreviated version of the interrupted scene that had just happened. It was only when she got to how Drew had stopped her that Keri reacted.

"Whoa, what a minute," Keri said. "You're telling me he stopped you? No wonder you're freaking out. That's when a girl's most vulnerable."

"I know!" Alexa beat her hand against the bedspread then winced and scrunched it up instead. "And what's worse, even though he's gorgeous and can cook and I'm so grateful for his protection, he's only ever discussed martial arts and our schools' rivalry when he knew I was turned on and not thinking straight. Maybe it's just this stalker situation getting to me, but would I be super paranoid to think it was possible that Drew was using me and this situation to manipulate a better business arrangement?"

Keri was silent for a long breath. "Yes. And no. It seems super unlikely, but stranger things have happened. Stranger things *are* happening."

"Exactly," Alexa said. "I just can't tell what's going on or what he's in this for."

"So don't decide now," Keri said. "I know it'll be hard, but maybe you can put the brakes on things. Drew already tried to. Just keep your distance—emotionally, at least."

"Yeah." Alexa's heart warned her that would be difficult.

Keri continued. "The bottom line? You're telling me you don't trust him. And that's a big deal, since you need trust if you're going to go forward in a relationship."

Alexa was silent, thinking on that. Keri was so right—again. She simply could not enter a relationship with someone if she was suspicious of him and wary of being manipulated. That was the height of folly. And it was most likely how so many of the second chances she'd seen implode went bad.

"You okay?" Keri asked.

"I'm better than okay," Alexa said. "I know what to do. Thanks, Keri. You're the best—with double-fudge and a cherry on top!"

Keri laughed. "Hey, always. But if you're good, I've got another call coming in. The world must sense I'm already awake."

Alexa signed off with Keri then lay back for a minute and closed her eyes. Trust—that was what she'd been missing. Drew had always been able to get beneath her skin, but that only meant he was more dangerous—her own particular brand of kryptonite. She would slow down, step back, and keep him at arm's length until her life returned to normal.

And for that, she needed the right clothes and makeup so she could feel truly like herself before she faced him again. None of this snuggling in pajamas in Drew's bed! She'd taken care of herself for a very long time without any help from a man. She would simply go back to that independence—no matter what her bonks and bruises said, and no matter that it was sometime after three o'clock in the morning.

Making a careful evaluation of the clothes that had thankfully never been removed from the guest bedroom closet, Alexa chose a pair of charcoal slacks and a pale-blue turtleneck. From the sounds of the storm outside, it was going to be a weary and wet night, followed by a morning of the same. She draped the clothes over her arm then headed into the bathroom. She was grateful for the sturdy lock on the bathroom door and felt a flicker of satisfaction as she slid it home. Being a guest in Drew's home definitely complicated her ability to take a firm stance. It would be good to get back in her own home and her own space. She wasn't normally the kind of girl who would throw herself at a guy. She turned the faucet to a comfortable heat and got undressed, using a washcloth to give herself a careful sponge bath.

She still could not believe Drew had pulled the plug on things like that. What was wrong with him? Maybe he was acting out some Special Forces honor code—no sex with the subject while he was protecting her. The trouble with that was, he'd been ready enough to tumble around on the dojo floor the other day and kiss her the night before that.

Alexa shook her head and would have screamed if she were sure the bathroom door would cover the sound. It just wasn't fair. How was she ever going to know if she could trust him? She could happily strangle him right now if only she dared put her hands on him.

But she didn't have to touch him, didn't have to deal with this. In a few hours, all of this nonsense with Stuart would be cleared up, and she could go home and forget Drew Cosimo even existed if she chose. Her one hope was that he was as ready to back off as she was.

As she gently combed out her hair, she tried to picture herself at home in her cozy little house, surrounded by her cats and her peaceful life. She wasn't able to feel the quickening joy she usually felt at that mental image. Instead, she felt her eyes fill with hot tears, but she blinked them away and told herself it was nothing but the pain of her head injury and all the strain she'd been under, plus the car accident. Was it any wonder she felt weepy, even at the thought of going home?

When she felt clean and tidy, Alexa swept her hair up into a soft bun, with feathery strands falling from the top of the bun to soften the back. It was one of her most professional looks, the one she reserved for meetings with the city when the library needed funding for a special project. Now she would use it to help her feel calm and cool around Drew.

Getting the turtleneck on was a trick, but it had a loose neck, and she managed it. With the slacks, she paired a conservative pair of camelbacks then started on her makeup. This was the most critical part. She wanted to hide her bruises—and her vulnerability—without looking done up. She definitely didn't want to look as though she were trying to catch Drew's eye.

When she finished, she stepped back and took a look at herself. The edges of the mirror were still fogged over, so the effect was a little more ethereal than she was going for, but she looked good—smart, sophisticated, and nobody's fool.

Now she just had to live up to the look. She opened the bathroom door and turned resolutely toward the main rooms of the house. As tempting as it was to hide in her room, she wanted to make perfectly clear to Drew that she wasn't emotionally dependent on him and wouldn't be swayed by him. She didn't have long until Stuart would be in custody, and she wanted to make the most of it by showing Drew the kind of relationship he could expect to have with her once she left—a friendship that was pleasantly professional.

CHAPTER EIGHTEEN

A S SHE STEPPED INTO THE kitchen, Alexa realized two things. The first was that she was starving. The smell of toasted cheese and something tantalizing that she couldn't quite name assaulted her senses. Her appetite pounced on the scent and deducted that something so delicious could only mean one thing—Drew was cooking. Her traitorous stomach was quick to remind Alexa that she'd only had soup for dinner last night and had pretty much skipped yesterday's lunch. It also reminded her that she never had food this good when she cooked for herself.

She realized that her pose as a frost maiden had just sustained its first serious assault. The doors to the library stood half open, welcoming her into the realm of books and cozy nooks. The heavenly smell came from in there, as did the flicker of reflected firelight.

Alexa followed the wonderful aroma, walking as if her feet were possessed of their own mind. She pushed open the door and paused just inside.

Drew had lit a fire and placed candles along the table running along the back of the couch. He'd centered a small round table and two chairs in front of the fire. On the table, a fancy wine bottle kept company with a tall flickering candle. Two places were set, and on each plate was Alexa's all-time favorite breakfast food—eggs benedict.

Alexa had to swallow around a suddenly tight throat. She drifted toward the table and looked down. It was her favorite dish. But his making it felt all wrong.

Drew stepped out of the shadows, a look of glimmering hope on his face. He was dressed in a nice pair of slacks and a deep-blue shirt that shimmered in the light. He looked positively scrumptious.

"What made you decide to fix this?" Alexa asked.

Drew's smile grew stronger. "You once said it was the way to your heart. I figured, given the circumstances, it was the least I could do."

Alexa couldn't breathe around the emotions rising inside her. She was trapped by the look in his eyes and by her own wash of emotion. One tear escaped her, and she swiped at it with a trembling hand. How had he backed her into a corner so quickly? And how did he know to make eggs benedict... wait. Dimly, the memory came back.

Years ago, she and Drew had been at a party when the subject of romantic dinners had come up, and how a guy should propose. The girls and guys had gotten into a kind of competition as to who could come up with the most extravagant or unusual setting. When Drew had asked Alexa for her input, she'd said that so long as there were candles burning, a fire lit, and eggs benedict for breakfast, the guy couldn't go wrong. At the time, Drew had teased her, then he'd forgotten about it—or so she'd thought.

"Alexa?" Drew reached a hand toward her, love evident on his face and in his eyes as they met hers.

The rest of her control dissolved. A torrent of tears stormed inside. She turned and ran—away from Drew and his preposterous, even traitorous, proposal, away from her pain, and away from her own feelings for him. Unfortunately, she was in his house, so running just highlighted how trapped she was.

She dodged the kitchen table and just missed slamming into the counter. As she rounded the corner and started down the hall to the guest bedroom, she made a sharp turn and headed toward the garage instead. She'd come back too quickly. Clearly aiming for friendly professionalism was a fool's hope—and everything in her revolted at being made the fool again.

The garage was shadowy and cold, even with the light on, and the heavy pounding of rain was louder out here. For just a second, she paused on the steps. Was this wise? No. But she was more afraid of what was behind her than anything in front of her.

She hurried down the steps and rushed to the truck. It wasn't until she was inside with the door slammed shut and fishing for keys that she realized her mistake. There were no keys, because this was Drew's truck. Her own little car was smashed up somewhere in a junkyard, a casualty to her deranged stalker.

She laid her head down on the steering wheel and cried.

How long she cried, she wasn't sure. Long enough to let her grief over her car—silly as that seemed—and her general frustrations out. Long enough to not even know what she was crying for anymore.

A gentle tapping on the truck's window brought her back to herself. She sniffed and applied another napkin to her nose, because apparently a Ranger's truck didn't come equipped with tissues. She didn't exactly look at Drew, who was waiting on the other side of the glass, but she turned her head enough to let him know she was listening.

He said something, but what it was didn't translate through the window. He waited, held up a set of keys, then raised his eyebrows as if to ask if she would like them.

Alexa hesitated then flipped the lock so he could open the door, and held out her hand.

Slowly, Drew opened the door, as if afraid she might jump out and run off. He rested the keys in her palm. He had to speak over the sound of the rain pelting the garage roof, and his voice was thickened by emotion. "I'm giving these to you, so you can leave if you want to. But I'm asking you to hear me out first."

Alexa swallowed and isolated one word in her swimming thoughts. "Okay."

Drew let go of the keys and took his hand back. Alexa shut the door, locked it, then put the keys in the ignition and rolled the window down. However, she left the engine off. Her urge to run was strong, but her desire to stay was stronger.

Drew took a deep breath and spoke clearly but gently. "I didn't mean to upset you in there. I wasn't thinking of how it would look. I'd forgotten the rest of the conversation at that party when you said you liked eggs benedict. I just remembered that it was a food you really liked, so I made it this morning as a comfort food for you."

Alexa's insides went still, almost as if all of her had become her ears and she was listening with even the pores of her skin.

Drew scrubbed a hand across his face. "I wasn't trying to propose. I wouldn't do that to you—not now and not so quickly. That would be a really jerkish thing to do, given what else is going on in your life right now. I'm sorry I upset you."

Alexa nodded. "That's okay." She blew out a breath. "I'm sorry I fell apart."

Drew waved a hand. "Don't be. You had every reason to fall apart, and you've actually held up amazingly." He grinned. "Worthy of a Ranger."

Alexa smiled back at him, albeit a bit wobbly. She looked down at the steering wheel and around the cab of the truck. It was tidy without being fussy and had a distinctive "Drew" scent that she found comforting, even now.

Something shifted inside, and without thinking that shift through, she looked back at Drew. "You said that you wouldn't do that—wouldn't propose—right now. Would you... do you think you will someday?"

Hope bloomed in Drew's eyes, and she had her answer right there. However, there was something else in his expression—caution.

Her question and the moment hung between them.

Drew's phone rang, and a look of relief washed over him. He signaled that he needed to get this and turned away to answer it.

Alexa rested her head on the back of the seat and closed her eyes for a second. It had been crazy for her to ask him that. Her thoughts were total nonsense. She was so tired—physically and emotionally. Her head throbbed where she'd been knocked out, and the rest of the aches and pains she'd acquired in the accident clamored loudly. She needed another painkiller. But what about her heart? It wasn't hurting. It didn't ache the way it had all morning. It wasn't throbbing like it had when Drew rebuffed her upstairs. She wasn't sure just what to make of all this, but her heart had quite suddenly decided it was just fine.

Something in Drew's tone changed as he talked on the phone. Alexa sat up and looked at him. He'd turned back toward her and the truck, and his eyes met hers. She read something in them that almost looked like—fear? He spoke into the phone, loud enough for Alexa to hear. "Got it. I'll get things squared away. Here's Alexa."

He held the phone out to Alexa, offering it through the truck window. "It's Detective Rawlings. She has something she wants to tell you directly."

Alexa nodded and took the phone gingerly. "Hello?"

"I'm glad you're up," Detective Rawlings said. Alexa could hear the sound of a siren in the background. "We've had a development."

"What's going on?" Alexa tried to speak calmly, as if she hadn't been a quivering emotional wreck five minutes ago. She was grateful that the truck's interior made it easy to hear the detective, despite the growing storm.

"The good news is we found evidence linking Stuart to the crimes—an online receipt where he purchased the eavesdropping device. And one of our guys lifted a print from the driver's side seat adjustment on the van he stole."

"Okay, that's good. Right?" Alexa braced herself mentally and emotionally, because there seemed to be a big unspoken "but" coming on the heels of Detective Rawlings's words. She used her free hand to turn the key in the ignition and rolled the window up. Then she cut the power, got out of the truck, and handed the keys back to Drew. Whatever it was she sensed was coming, she knew in her gut she wouldn't survive it without Drew at her back. She pressed the phone tight to her ear.

Detective Rawlings's voice was grim. "Yes, but unfortunately, we were unable to pick him up at his house. It looks like he hasn't been living there. He's got a second property—a storage place, really—that he rents. We're getting a warrant to check the premises and see if we can find anything that will lead us to him."

"So, he's still out there." Alexa still felt as if she was waiting for the other shoe to drop. Sure, she'd been in an accident and had a long couple of days, but why didn't Detective Rawlings get to the point?

"That's right." Detective Rawlings paused, and Alexa wondered if her lungs would explode from holding her breath. "The trouble is, we found a paper at his house. It has a formula on it for a fairly powerful fire accelerant, so we believe he may be planning arson. It also has four addresses on it—your house, Crouching Tiger, Drew's MMA studio, and your friend Keri's place."

Alexa sucked in air so fast, her head did a dizzy swirl. "Keri's place?" she heard herself ask. Without even registering what she was doing, she stepped closer to Drew. He put his arm around her and guided her up the garage stairs, into the house, and to a seat on the couch.

"Yes, but I've spoken with her on the phone. I've also sent two officers over there to move Keri somewhere safe until we catch up to Stuart. The other places on the list will be watched as well, and I'm sending a pair of uniforms out to stay with you two. Hang tight for now, stay inside, and I'll be phoning you soon to say we've got him."

"But it doesn't make sense." Alexa's brain was stuck several sentences back. "Why would he put Keri's house on the list? He knows I'm not staying there. And I just talked to her. Did her house go on the list because I called her?"

"No, this list was made some time ago—of that, I'm sure." The phone was muffled for a moment while Detective Rawlings spoke to someone else, then she was back on the line with Alexa. "He may have put Keri's house on the list when he thought you were there. The list itself may also be nothing more than a scare tactic or a maneuver to buy him time. We'll get answers soon. Stay close to Drew, stay inside, and keep your guard up."

Detective Rawlings hung up, and Alexa handed the phone to Drew.

He shook his head. "Keep it." He walked to the door, locked it, and now he pulled her up to walk beside him as he made a thorough and careful inspection of each door and window. Outside, the storm rattled and raged.

Trailing him and watching him work efficiently to protect her, Alexa felt a stone settle on her heart. They'd come close to something this morning—some understanding. But her situation and the threat of her stalker had once again inserted itself. Would she have been able to follow that lead if Stuart's sick obsession hadn't interrupted them? She didn't know. She was worried that Stuart would hurt Keri or someone else, that Drew would use her to blight the good things she was doing at

Crouching Tiger, that he would simply break her heart. Would she ever be free of fear again?

"Hey, come here." Drew took her in his arms. "The police know who they're looking for and have their best people focused on bringing Stuart in. It's going to be okay."

Alexa didn't have the heart to tell him Stuart wasn't the only person she was afraid of at the moment. She didn't like misleading him, or leading him on, or whatever this was, and was stiff for two seconds. But she couldn't resist his hug and quickly melted into his arms. It was funny—he was one of her fears, yet when he put his arms around her, all the fears faded, and she felt safe.

Drew turned his face into her hair and sniffed appreciatively then kissed her head. "Come on." He released her. "Let's get up to the safe room. We can wait there for Detective Rawlings's call."

Get up to the safe room… he thinks Stuart might try to break in. The fear tried to fountain up at that thought, but Alexa pushed it aside.

"What about my cats?" she asked. "Do we have time to get them?"

"We'll gather Oreo and Ragbag," Drew said decisively. "Fieldgar is still upstairs. The last thing we need is Stuart having leverage over us because your cats aren't safe. But we need to be quick."

Alexa gulped and nodded. They'd already seen that he was more than happy to threaten her fur babies.

Drew shadowed her as she headed toward the guest bedroom. He checked each room briefly before she entered it, and he had produced a handgun from somewhere. Alexa wanted to ask how long he'd been carrying, but she didn't want to distract either of them with idle chitchat.

A quick search turned up Oreo, but no Ragbag.

Alexa clutched her black-and-white kitty and tried not to hyperventilate. This was precisely the point in a horror movie when the bad guy would get them—while they were searching for the lost cat.

Drew rubbed a hand on her back, bringing her a bit of calm. "Let's check the library. I think he may have followed you in earlier but not back out."

Alexa nodded and headed in that direction, carrying Oreo. It was kind of Drew to not mention her having run out of there, but it was still embarrassing to walk back in, given that she'd completely flipped just because he made her a delicious eggs dish.

She stopped at the entrance to the library. The candles had been snuffed out, and the romantic atmosphere had evaporated. The eggs were congealed in their sauce. However, Ragbag was curled up in front of the mostly dead fire.

"There you are." Alexa smiled at Drew in her relief. She passed him Oreo then picked up Ragbag, and they both headed upstairs.

They'd just stepped inside the bedroom when the lights went out.

In the sudden darkness, the flash of lightning and the boom of thunder that followed felt loud enough to wake the dead.

CHAPTER NINETEEN

REW HEARD ALEXA GASP, AND his own gut clenched with fear. The two minutes it took until the automatic generator kicked in seemed to drag. Even after the lights flickered and came back on, Drew couldn't relax. Had the storm knocked out the power, or had that been Stuart's doing?

He set the cat down and quickly bolted the doors behind Alexa and him. Then he double-checked that all the rooms—master bath, bedroom, and closets—were clear of intruders and secure.

Alexa didn't say anything, just clutched her phone and her cat. So Drew tried to help her relax a bit. "There's a whole-house generator outside in a locked cabinet, so we have power. We'll be safe in here." He double-checked the bedroom door leading to the hall as he continued. "See the bolts at the top and bottom of this door? They slide deep into a reinforced solid wood frame, and the flimsy original door has been exchanged for a solid outer door. As an added bonus, all the windows are reasonably shatterproof." He chuckled, the sound coming out mostly normal. "I'm glad, now, that I decided to try out this plan so I could recommend it to students. I never thought then that I'd need to use it."

He looked at Alexa, hoping she would find that amusing, but she was sitting on the chair Drew had used when he watched over her, staring straight ahead.

"Alexa?" Had Drew's idle comments about security worried her?

"Why would he put Keri on the list?" Alexa asked, as if Drew hadn't spoken. Her face was pale. "He must have known I wasn't staying with her. She lives in town, so he could easily watch to see if I was going in and out. Why would he go after her?"

Her voice caught on the last word. That plus the pale color of her skin and the way she'd tugged her sleeves down to keep her hands warm told him one thing—in the face of the emotional shock and physical stress she'd been under, her body was struggling to keep all functions going.

He went to the bed and snagged a blanket off it then tucked it around her. Alexa clung to his hands as he smoothed the folds out of the blanket, so he sat down across from her on the bed, where he could warm her fingers with his.

"My guess is he was acting out a need to control you," Drew said, thinking it through as he spoke. "He may have planned to use an attack on Keri to get to you, draw you out. Or use the threat of hurting her to make you do what he asked."

"It would have worked too." Alexa shivered and lowered her head to his hands. "I just can't believe this—and yet I do believe it. It's real. And it's all my fault."

"What?" Drew pulled Alexa's chin up so he could look in her eyes. "This is not your fault, not in any way. Why would you believe that?"

Alexa shook her head, and tears welled in her eyes. "I remembered something from the day a couple weeks ago when Stuart had his argument with Master Hays. I watched the whole thing 'cause Master Hays and I had been going over preparations for the next day's classes when it started. Stuart was pushing the master to let him test on the next exam date, but Master Hays said he wasn't ready. Told him he hadn't mastered the control needed for an advanced belt. After the argument, Master Hays went into the office, and Stuart went to get his stuff. On the way out the door, he passed me, and I put my hand out to touch his arm. Stuart's not all bad, and I just wanted him to know he was still welcome in the dojo. I said something like 'see you next time,' and he went out the door."

"But how does that—" Drew started.

"Just listen!" Alexa gulped in a breath and brushed angrily at the tears on her cheeks. "The next time he came in was for sparring class, and I was on the floor, fighting as team captain. He was on the other team, but he came to stand by my group. He kept kind of jostling them, egging them on, as if he thought he was in charge of them and it was his job to razz them. I tried to keep my cool and tell him off politely, but he responded to my comments as if I were just some twit and he didn't have to listen to me. He was really rude and even crude but did it in a way that made the offense mostly inflection. Clever and sneaky."

Alexa looked up, and Drew could see the gleam of anger in her eyes. "Quite frankly, it pissed me off. Especially when he then turned around and gave Brianna a bad time when she made a mistake that cost her the match. So I paired myself against Stuart and quite literally knocked him on his butt. I usually hold back against lower belts. There's no point in showing off, you know? But I just let him have it. I don't think he scored a single point, and the fight was over in less than three minutes."

"Must have been quite the sight," Drew said. "I wish I could have seen it." He meant it too. Watching Alexa clean up on a bully like Stuart would have been worth any admission price.

"But don't you see?" Alexa cried. "That's probably why he came after me—where this obsession and need to control me came from. I sent him confusing signals, and he lost it."

"No, you've got it all wrong." Somehow Drew had to convince her that shouldering a burden of guilt wouldn't make the situation any better. "You showed compassion for him and acted the part of the good instructor when he got reamed out and wasn't allowed to test. Then when he acted like a jerk, you took him down a peg. The only way this is your fault is if it's the job of the whole world to walk softly around bullies and pacify them every time they throw a tantrum."

Alexa looked down, her hands clenching and unclenching the blanket. "What if I took out my anger at Jason Stone on him? I've had that problem before when guys acted like jerks. Kind of made them pay a little extra, because Jason hurt my friend and scared me so bad. As if kicking them extra hard will prevent them from hurting anyone in the future."

Drew shook his head. "No way could you have created this whole scale. The Stuart I know was already capable of being an extreme jerk. You didn't cause this."

Alexa nodded, but her face remained troubled. "But if I had kept my temper, gone a little easier on him in the fight—"

"Odds are he would have acted exactly the same way." Drew brought his hand up to cup Alexa's cheek. "Regardless of what mistakes you may have made, you couldn't know he was a psycho, and you couldn't anticipate how exactly he was going to go crazy. Nor was it your job to smooth his path and keep him from jumping over that edge. Stuart made his own choices, and you are not in any way responsible for his actions."

Alexa nodded, but Drew wasn't sure if she actually understood and agreed with him or if she was just letting it go. He would've liked to have pressed the issue, but just then, the phone rang.

Alexa held up the phone so he could see the screen. It was Detective Rawlings. The gut-clenching nerves he felt were reflected in Alexa's eyes as she swiped the screen and put the call on speaker before she answered. "Hello?"

"The two of you need to move somewhere else." Detective Rawlings's tone was urgent, and she spoke over the sound of a siren. "Watch your back but get out. Stuart's at your house, and he's going to burn it down with you inside."

A jolt of adrenaline slammed through Drew, bringing his senses to high alert and his mind into sharp focus. He could feel himself switch into Ranger mode, and his voice came out clipped and nearly emotionless. "What's the situation?" he asked Detective Rawlings. "How long until backup arrives?"

"It'll be at least twenty minutes." Detective Rawlings's voice was charged with frustrated tension. "Stuart felled trees across the only road in to your place. They're just this side of the bridge and completely blocking the road. We've got some guys gearing up to walk in, but we figure it will be twenty minutes before anyone reaches the house. Longer if the guys on foot take any fire—we believe Stuart to be armed."

Alexa sucked in a breath, and Drew gave her hand a squeeze before answering. "My truck's not four-wheel drive. If Stuart's here, why wouldn't he try to negotiate? We have the safe room. We can wait it out." The police were just assuming Stuart was there to burn the house.

He could have just as easily downed the trees in order to scare them out of the house and ambush them while they were out in the open.

"No, his tactic has changed. He's not here to negotiate, and the accelerant he's using burns fast," Detective Rawlings said. "We lost Alexa's house. The fire was out of control before the fire department got there. It looks like they'll save Crouching Tiger, but damages will be heavy. If he gets a fire started on your house, you'll be gone before we can get the road cleared and a fire truck through."

Drew looked quickly at Alexa. She'd sucked in a breath, her eyes glazing as if she could see the fires burning. The bandage on her head stood out against her pale skin.

Drew lifted a hand to cup her cheek comfortingly before taking the phone and turning off speaker. He spoke grimly. "Then I'd better make sure he doesn't get a fire going." Detective Rawlings tried to protest, but he cut her off. "See you in twenty minutes." He hung up the phone and put his arms around Alexa in a hug because she looked as though she would fall over without one, then reached down and pulled out his Glock from his ankle holster. "Do you know how to use a gun?"

Alexa shook her head and raised her hands in a gesture of refusal. "I shot skeet a couple times as a kid, but the only time I tried to use a handgun, I nearly shot the instructor. And doesn't that kind kick? You should keep it."

"A shotgun would be a good idea." Drew worked the slide on the Glock and checked the magazine. "I'll look into getting one after this is over. For now, take this and just remember to hold it firmly with both hands. Point directly at the target, fire two shots at a time, and keep your thumb out of the way of the slide."

"No, Drew, I'm not taking it," Alexa said with a hard shake of her head. She stood. "You're not giving me your backup. Not when you're going out there to... to face a psychotic madman. Besides, it won't do me any good."

"I'll make do, Alexa." Drew stood as well, anxious to go find Stuart. He was tempted to just leave it on the bed, where she would have to take it. "That's what a Ranger does. You need to be armed."

"I don't want it," Alexa insisted, her voice wobbling a bit as it rose.

"I know enough about guns to know I'm better off without one than trying to use something I don't understand. What if Stuart took it away from me while I was fumbling around and used it on me?" When Drew still hesitated, she pushed him away. "Go. At this rate, Stuart will have the house on fire before you've left the bedroom."

Drew nodded. Maybe she was right. The first rule was to never hold a gun unless you were prepared to use it, and this wasn't the time for a crash course with the Glock. If he did his job properly, Stuart would never get the fire started, and Alexa would be safe in the bedroom until the police arrived.

"Stay inside and don't open the door unless you're absolutely sure it's me. Remember, a safe room is only as secure as its weakest point, and in this room, that's the door." Drew allowed himself one moment to cup Alexa's cheek, then he strode to the door. "I'll wait right outside until you tell me you have the locks secure." He slipped out the bedroom door. It was time to stop Stuart once and for all.

CHAPTER TWENTY

A LEXA CLOSED THE DOOR BEHIND Drew and pushed the deadbolts in place. She slapped the door twice. "All set."

Drew slapped the door back once. A minute or two later, she heard the front door open and close downstairs.

Suddenly feeling very alone, Alexa went to the bed and climbed up to reach the crossed bo staffs that were resting on hooks in the wall. Drew may have considered them to be a kind of warrior design statement, but to her practiced eye, they looked like serviceable weapons. If Stuart poked his head in the door, she would bash it in.

A rattle of pounding rain hit the windows, and Alexa jumped. The storm that had been rising all night was finally letting loose the full torrent of its fury.

She went to the window and looked out. There was no sign of the sun rising. She should have reminded Drew to take a jacket. He was going to get soaked. On the other hand, the lashing rain ought to make it harder for Stuart to get a fire going. At least, she hoped it would. She didn't know how his fire accelerant worked.

An image of Stuart in the rain, his long, stringy moustache flying, while he tried over and over to strike a match came to mind. A bubble of hilarity rose inside Alexa, and a fit of insane giggles cramped her stomach. Fighting them had her almost doubled in half.

Alexa dropped down on the bed until the urge to laugh passed and found herself sobbing in its wake. Oh, this was bad. She really was losing it. There she was, trapped in Drew's bedroom behind barred doors, while he tromped around in the freezing rain and tried to watch all four sides of the house at once. Meanwhile, a twisted madman was doing everything he could to put them both in an early grave.

The rain rattled against the window again, and Alexa shivered. She pulled the throw off the bed and wrapped it around her shoulders. It smelled like Drew, and for just a split second, she felt a glow of warmth and safety in its embrace. That glow faded as she thought of the worry in Drew's eyes as he'd listened to Detective Rawlings tell them they had to leave. If something happened to him out there, she wasn't sure she could survive it. How could it be that she'd run away from him when she'd thought he was asking her to marry him, but ever since then, she'd felt disappointed that he wasn't?

She didn't understand how that was possible when earlier tonight she'd been ready to walk away from him for good. What was wrong with her, really? Was she broken in some way? Maybe that was why Stuart had been attracted to her. He'd seen that she wasn't capable of a real relationship and offered her the only alternative he could.

She shook her head, trying to toss that thought aside. No. Drew was right. It wasn't her fault that Stuart had become obsessed. That was what they taught women in their self-defense classes. A person was responsible for her own actions and their direct consequences but not another's choices. For example, if there really wasn't any way to know a guy was a psycho, then a woman couldn't be blamed for dating him. She would only be to blame if she went back to him—like Sierra had when she went back to Jason Stone. Except…

Alexa rubbed her hand across the bandage on her head, fighting a headache that wanted to blur her thoughts. Sierra hadn't known what Jason was capable of. Sure, they'd had a tumultuous relationship, but he'd never been violent, and he'd kept his past episodes of spiraling depression a secret. Had Alexa been blaming Sierra all these years for what happened in the bookstore that day? Just like she blamed herself for what Stuart was doing?

Alexa rose and paced the length of Drew's room then back again. She thought back over all her issues since that day in the bookstore. The inner turmoil had plagued her for months, if not years, afterward. Maybe she hadn't exactly been blaming Sierra, but she'd definitely tried to explain to herself what had happened to her friend in terms she could understand and, therefore, take steps to prevent anything like it from happening to her. She stopped in the middle of the room, her brain nearly exploding with the weight of her epiphany.

That was the reason she'd been so set against "reunion" relationships, against ever going back to a guy once things hadn't worked out the first time. She thought by avoiding the actions Sierra had taken, she could protect herself from the pain and helplessness she'd felt when her friend was attacked. Except the only thing her little safety rule had done was deny her the happiness of giving Drew a second chance. It had done nothing to protect her from Stuart's craziness.

Her rule was stupid. Alexa slashed the bo staff through the air then doubled it back in a move that would have cracked her opponent on the head and knocked him flat. Life couldn't be defined by a narrow set of rules, any more than someone could win a sparring match with a set combination of kicks and punches. Sure, there were guidelines—don't go home with strange guys, and don't trust a guy who's lied to you. But the big deciding moves required a willingness to trust your gut and take a leap of faith.

If Alexa stopped running from herself and faced her core feelings, she had to admit that if Drew were ever to ask her in the future if she would marry him, she would say yes. He'd proven himself trustworthy, and he'd apologized for any wrongdoing five years ago. She knew he was honorable. Moreover, she liked and trusted him… loved him, even.

Her heart leapt as those words entered her mind. A happy glow swelled inside her and made her want to hug herself or squee for joy!

Without thinking, she started toward the bedroom door. But Drew was long gone, out in the storm and darkness, hoping to catch Stuart before Stuart got to him.

Alexa swung back to face the windows, trying and failing to see anything in the blackness outside. It was as though all the light had been sucked out of the night, leaving only random flashes of lightning to tear the sky.

Against the reflected glass, she saw her memory of Stuart's face when he'd stopped to help her with her tire. She remembered the way his expression had changed when he'd seen Drew crossing the parking lot toward them.

Her blood chilled. Stuart had poked and pried into every secret corner of her life. He must know by now what Drew meant to her—even better than she did. The way Stuart had lit fire to her home and her dojo, and the way he'd gone after Keri's house... he didn't just want to control her. He wanted to hurt her. With that as his goal, wouldn't Drew make the best target?

The way that thought squeezed at her heart and made her sway on her feet only confirmed her guess. Now that she was being honest about how she felt, everything seemed obvious. Stuart hadn't come here to burn down Drew's house. That was just a way to smoke them out. He'd come here to kill Drew.

Alexa spun on the end of the bo staff and rushed to the door. She stopped with her hand on the lock, remembering Drew's words as he'd left. The safe room wasn't safe once she opened the door.

But how could she stay safely tucked away in there and let Drew walk into a trap? Detective Rawlings said Stuart was armed. He would be less likely to shoot her right away, but his whole purpose at this point was to kill Drew. No way could she let that happen.

Alexa yanked the door open and kept the bo staff ready as she slipped down the stairs. Every one of her senses was on high alert.

Something moved in the living room to her right. Alexa whirled, the bo staff zinging through the air.

She stopped short. It was only Ragbag, who must have followed her out of the bedroom. Alexa gave a half laugh, half sob of relief and reminded herself to calm down. She needed to get a grip. And she needed to hurry.

She stilled the impulse to grab Ragbag and rush him upstairs. The cats should be secure inside the house. If Stuart did start a fire, they would have a better chance of getting out if they were running free. Besides, she had no idea how much time she had to find Drew before Stuart did.

She dodged the pillows Fieldgar had knocked to the floor as she hurried through the living room. Then she let herself out through the library doors. She was hoping the side door into the garden would be less conspicuous. She locked the door behind herself then moved to her left, staying close to the house. She couldn't see anything in the dark and rain, but she was pretty sure Drew kept this side of the house mostly clear of plants. Some instinct told her that Stuart would be more likely to set his trap at the back of the house, out of sight of the road.

Her progress was slow in the darkness. She was also drenched by the time she got to the corner of the house. The rain ran like tears down her face. The one good thing about the storm was she didn't have to worry about how much noise she made. The thunder and wind covered up any small sounds. Of course, that also meant she wouldn't hear anyone creeping up on her.

Her mind supplied an image of Stuart, sneaking up behind her, an ugly look of triumph twisting his face. The picture was only in her mind, but it was real enough to make her heart start a pitter-patter of panicked drumbeats.

Crouching down next to the house, Alexa took a moment to breathe. *In and out.*

Her hands were trembling, but she tightened her grip on the bo staff and moved on. When she got to the back corner behind the garden, she peered cautiously around it. The kitchen light had been left on, making a bright square of yellow glow on the grass. It gave her a little light to see by, but it would also clearly outline her to any watchers if she tried to sneak past that part of the house. She would have to find a path that kept her out of the light. But where was Drew?

She stood still, watching the darkness and listening as hard as she could.

She'd just decided she was alone, when the sky was lit by a jagged streak of lightning. She gasped.

Standing across the open backyard, directly in front of her, was Stuart. He stood almost casually, leaning against a tree. His attention was focused on some point in front of him and to her left. He raised his arm, aiming a handgun with careful precision.

Alexa slapped her hand across her mouth to stifle a scream. She still didn't know where Drew was, but Stuart obviously did. But she didn't dare make a sound. If what Stuart wanted was to kill Drew, then he would just shoot him when he heard her scream a warning.

She swallowed her scream and backed quickly away from the corner of the house. She was going to have to circle around and come up behind Stuart without him seeing her—and she needed to do it fast.

Using the bo staff to help her find a path, she left the house and struck out into the surrounding forest. Branches whipped her face, and a couple of times, she almost lost her grip on the bo staff. She prayed the lightning wouldn't alert Stuart to her arrival before she was safely out of his sight.

She tried to keep a firm mental fix on the point where she'd seen Stuart. The square of light coming from the kitchen window helped. If she made a big loop around that point, she should come up somewhere behind Stuart.

Of course, it was the *somewhere* that was a problem.

She stopped and stood still, listening.

She twitched as a bright white light sliced through the darkness to her left.

The powerful beam cut through the darkness in a broad path, crossing the backyard. It came from an industrial spotlight resting on the ground, and it started maybe six feet to Alexa's left. The beam was pointed at a small shed that stood ten or fifteen feet across the backyard.

Drew knelt in the mud and rain behind the shed, bent over a small box. Wires ran from the box to the shed.

As the light fell across him, Drew pulled his gun from his shoulder holster and, in the same fluid movement, dove toward the edge of the light.

"Freeze!" Stuart shouted from where he stood in the shadows, just behind the spotlight. He fired off a shot inches from Drew's face, sending mud and dirt spraying in the air.

Drew froze. He squinted into the light, then he held his gun out from his body in a careful gesture of surrender and rolled slowly to his knees.

"Drop the gun," Stuart called.

Drew dropped the Glock in the dirt in front of him. He kept both hands up at shoulder height and nodded his head toward the box beside him. "Is this how you planned to burn down the house?" he called back.

Alexa nodded to herself. Drew was asking questions. That must mean he wanted Stuart to talk. She rested her cheek on the trunk of the tree next to her and held herself still so she wouldn't mess up his plan—and also so she could keep herself together.

Stuart's laugh rang out, sounding more than a little crazy. "That's nothing, just garbage. Bait to get you where I wanted you. This house isn't going to burn. Why would I burn down my new home? I don't want Alexa to pout."

Drew let out a bark of laughter. "She's not the pouting type, but you put a scratch on me, and I'm sure she'll kick your ass."

Alexa smiled.

Stuart took an aggressive step forward, closer to the light. "Alexa wouldn't dream of it, not when I'm done with her. We're going to live here, and she's going to clean the house for me, naked, on her hands and knees."

Drew jerked at those words, and Stuart laughed again. "Think on that, Drew boy. I want you to have that image burned into your thoughts when I blow your brains out."

Alexa eased back. Drew's plan was taking too long, if he even had one. It sounded as though Stuart was ready to shoot at any minute. She backed off another step or two, keeping the tree between her and Stuart. Once again, she made a small circle, but this time, she knew exactly where Stuart was, so she could come up directly behind him.

Stuart raised his gun a little higher, and even from a distance, Alexa could see the concern on Drew's face. Whether from the gun pointed at him or because he'd seen her, she didn't know. Drew opened his mouth, but Stuart spoke across him. "Say good-bye to your dreams, Drew. And say hello to your dick of a granddad for me."

Alexa wasn't quite in place, but it was now or never. She rushed forward, bringing the bo staff up and around in an overhead strike.

Her aim was true, but Stuart must have caught some flicker of motion.

He jerked away.

The staff glanced off the side of his head, with the tree trunk taking most of the blow.   Alexa jerked at the staff, but it snagged on a tree branch.

Stuart snaked out a hand and wrapped his fingers around her throat in a crushing grip. "Move, and your boyfriend gets it," he hissed.

Alexa froze, her eyes going to the gun. Stuart still had it up and pointed directly at Drew.

Stuart took advantage of her indecision to dig his fingers into the skin of her throat and drag her close. Alexa tried to get the staff clear so she could swing at his gun hand, but with the trees all around them, she was working in close quarters, and the bo was meant for open space. All she could do was thump him on the leg.

Stuart kicked the staff away and jerked her around so her back was to him. He cinched his arm in tight on her throat. Alexa's body shouted at her to use any of the many moves she knew to buy her space and get free. But her eyes went from Drew to the gun, and she held still.

Stuart chuckled, his breath stirring her hair. "So glad you joined us, Alexa. This hasn't really been my night, but you've gotten the party back on track."

Drew had one foot on the ground in what was almost a sprinter's stance and looked almost ready to bolt across the intervening space and tackle Stuart. But with the gun pointed right at him and a blinding light shining in his eyes, he must have known he wouldn't make it half that distance.

"What do you think, Drew?" Stuart called. "Shall I make her tie you up, then make you watch while I rape her? Or shall I make her watch me kill you, first?"

"Try either one, and you'll realize why Alexa's a black belt and you don't deserve the brown belt you have," Drew called.

There was something new to his tone, something intended for Alexa's ears. She turned her head to look at him directly, and he smiled encouragingly.

Stuart made a scoffing sound and tightened his hold on her throat. His arm was cutting into her windpipe, making her fight for air, but she held still. What was Drew signaling her to do?

"I'm an Army Ranger," Drew called, still seeming to speak to her. "Been around some pretty good fighters and seen some good moves. But the routine Alexa was working on for the grand opening of my school might be the best I've ever seen."

"Too bad she won't get to show it off," Stuart said. "Your grand opening will be rescheduled as your funeral." His arm clenched even tighter, but Alexa didn't mind. She knew what Drew was asking. He wanted her to do the move she'd used on him when she flipped him in the dojo. But could she pull it off? When Drew taught it to her, he hadn't been holding a gun, and no one's life had been on the line if she made a mistake.

Stuart made the decision for her. His head shifted just a bit to the left, and Alexa realized he was taking more careful aim.

In a quick succession of practiced moves, she tucked her hips and hunched her body, closing the gap between her and Stuart. Her hand clamped down on the arm he had wound around her neck to keep it in place and give her better leverage. She shifted her hips and leaned forward, lifting Stuart's weight onto her back, then threw her upper body toward her knees as though she were heading into a somersault. His arm was so tight around her neck, it felt as if he were going to take her head with him, but he came free as she started to flip him.

Stuart flipped over her right shoulder and landed in the beam from the spotlight he'd trained on Drew.

Alexa heard shots, and for a sickening moment, she was sure she'd failed. Stuart had shot Drew despite her throw.

Then her senses settled, and the ground stopped whirling. Drew was still kneeling by the outbuilding. His pant leg was pulled up, and he had his Glock in his hand.

Stuart lay where she'd thrown him, blood spreading in a pool beneath him.

Alexa stared at the blood, her brain fixed on the sight. She raised her hand to push her wet hair out of her eyes, but her hand was shaking so badly, she hit herself in the face.

Drew rushed over to her. "Are you hurt?" His hands slid over her, checking for damage.

Alexa shook her head numbly.

Drew checked Stuart's pulse and shook his head.

"He's…?" The question died in Alexa's bruised throat.

Drew nodded then stood and pulled out his phone. He looked at Alexa while he dialed. "He shot first, you understand? I wouldn't have shot him otherwise."

Alexa broke free of her numbness to nod and put her arms around Drew. He tucked her close while he talked on the phone with the dispatcher. When he hung up, he walked her to the house, keeping her feet moving in the right direction when they strayed.

The next hour was a blur for Alexa. There were police everywhere and questions to be answered. Detective Rawlings checked on her several times, and Drew stayed with her every minute he could. EMTs examined her and talked with Drew about what she needed. Everyone was very patient, and Alexa tried to keep herself alert. She needed to talk to Drew, needed to tell him she loved him. But the last few days had finally caught up to her.

She woke when Drew lifted her and carried her upstairs. She wasn't usually big on being carried, but it felt so good to rest in his arms. And he carried her so easily, she felt as though she could stay there forever. She looked up into Drew's face. His hair had been toweled dry but was still wet, and he had dark, glistening curls on his forehead. His eyes were tired but filled with love. Such a wonderful face, and such a dear man. Every day for the rest of her life, Alexa would be grateful he was okay. Her heart was still ready to leap and run when she thought about that awful moment when she heard the shots and thought it had been him.

"Drew," Alexa murmured, reaching up to touch his cheek. "I love you."

Drew stumbled, looking down at her with wonder. He shook his head in bewilderment and hitched her a little higher in his arms. "Maybe I'd better call the EMTs back, have them check you again. You're talking crazy."

Alexa laughed, the sound bubbling out of her. "It's true! Honest to goodness. That's why I came out, because I knew Stuart would go after you."

Drew shook his head again, but his eyes were bright with joy. He gripped her a little tighter and planted a kiss on an unbruised bit of her forehead as he crossed the bedroom.

He set her on the bed then knelt beside her and held her close. His warm, loving eyes held hers. His voice was gentle but filled with conviction. "I love you, Alexa."

Alexa smiled, and for a moment, she just let herself drift on the love in his eyes. She was ready to fall asleep again, but there was something else she wanted to say. What was it?

Oh yeah. She struggled up on her elbows so she could look at Drew directly. "And the other thing? If you ever decide to make me eggs benedict again, my answer is yes."

Drew laughed, a delighted sound. "Then I'll have to make them soon." He leaned in to kiss her tenderly. After lingering on her lips for just a minute, he drew back. "Are you sure? This isn't just a post-trauma reaction?"

Alexa sighed and drew him close again so she could snuggle into him. She rested her head on his chest while she talked. "I think I've always loved you. I just didn't know it. I was hung up on that whole situation with Sierra and Jason Stone—the guy who attacked my friend that day at the bookstore. I'm not sure how everything got blurred together in my brain..."

She drifted to a halt for a second, thinking about that. "I was so angry when you left, and I thought you didn't care. I tried to go out with other guys, but I couldn't pretend they mattered like you had. I'd just about resigned myself to hoping you'd come home on break sometime. I thought I'd forgive you, and we'd hit it off. I hated myself for that hope. Then Jason's attack on Sierra happened. Somehow, my hurt and helplessness after the attack got blended in my mind with the hurt I felt toward you, and I decided I'd never, ever let you in and corner myself like that."

Drew's face was sober as she finished. "I'm sorry that experience was so painful. I'm sorry I hurt you when I left."

Alexa smiled up at him. "None of it was your fault, not really. And anyway, we both had growing up to do before we could come back together." She quirked an eyebrow at him. "It says a lot that you're willing to forgive me for all the things I've said about you since you came back to Willowdale. You do realize half the town will fall over in a faint when they realize we're dating?"

Drew laughed. "Let them swoon. Besides, when they see how well we work together at my open house, they'll realize it was meant to be."

"Meant to be," Alexa repeated, snuggling down in the blankets again. She gave Drew's hand a tug so he would lie beside her in the bed. "I like the sound of that."

Drew stretched out beside her, his long frame spooning her and giving her a deeply satisfying feeling of comfort. His arms wrapped around her body, and his breath stirred her hair when he spoke. "Good night, my beautiful Alexa. Sweet dreams."

Alexa closed her eyes and let her senses open to the closeness of Drew. She smiled, the gladness going all through her. This moment was worth everything that had come before it. Her nightmare was over, and her heart had come home.

ACKNOWLEDGEMENTS

I have been fortunate to gain writing friends who feel like family over the years, so I must send my love to my writing sisters Erica Christensen, Laura Andersen, Pat Esden, Ginger Churchill, and Becca Fitzpatrick. Thank you so much for all the hugs, love, encouragement, and chocolate over the years. I never could have done it without you!

Many thanks to my two 'first' writing mentors, Caleb Warnock and James Maxey. You shone a light down the path, helping me push forward when the way was hard to see.

A huge thank you to Jessica Anderegg and Neila Forssberg for their unwavering dedication and patience in helping this book to become a reality, and to the rest of the Red Adept team, especially Lynn McNamee, who runs the ins and outs of publishing with poise, grace, and an uncanny savvy. And also to all my fellow Red Adept authors. I've benefitted so much from all your wisdom and insights!

A gigantic hug of thanks to my sisters, Joy Hopper, Karin Joyce and Liza Edgell, for all your support in helping me get here, and also a particular thank you to my brother, Sgt. Jake Warnock, for going above and beyond in answering random texts and odd phone calls with questions about military life.

I must also acknowledge a debt to the various writing organizations from which I've benefitted over the years while writing this book and others, such as SCBWI, SFWA, and especially Romance Writers of America. I've found the workshops and conferences I've attended to be universally helpful.

In an endeavor like this, spanning years, there are so many wonderful people who play a part in shaping the writer and the book. Accordingly, I want to thank Orson Scott Card and my boot camp buddies, the wonderful folk in the Authors Think Tank, my writing pals in the NC Kidlit group, and the many other amazing author friends I have made over the years, plus my wonderful supporters in Northern Virginia and in the Hillsborough, Durham, and Raleigh, NC, communities that have nurtured me and my family over the years. Thank you so much for your smiles, encouragement, and support. I wish I could reach out and give each and every one of you a hug, because each of you played a significant role in this book's creation.

A special thank you to the folk of TKD Martial Arts Academy of Burke, VA, for pushing me to my limits in pursuit of my black belt, and for being my first martial arts family. In particular I want to thank my black belt instructors for their patience and dedication in sharing a love of martial arts with the young, old, and in between and for treating each student with dignity.

I also want to thank my mom-in-law, Karen Peterson, for her many years of enthusiastic support and faith in me, and extend that thanks to the entire wonderful family that I gained by marriage.

And finally, sincere thanks and love to my sweet husband, Chad, and my two kids, Jeremiah and Rianna. We've spent what feels like a lifetime on this journey of publication together—thanks so much for being the best possible traveling companions I could ever have.

ABOUT THE AUTHOR

Lily Black believes in true love, but she is also quite certain that going after it is the scariest thing we'll ever do. She explores this dynamic in her romantic suspense novels, which are set in the small imaginary town of Willowdale, where people dream big, love deeply, and kick butt if necessary.

Lily has a black belt in Chung Do Kwan Tai Kwon Do, and she has also trained in everything from judo to broadswords. She lives in North Carolina, where she tries to divide her free time between the mountains and the sea. She shares her home with a very patient and loving husband and their teenage daughter.

www.ingramcontent.com/pod-product-compliance
Lightning Source LLC
Chambersburg PA
CBHW030349200626
46808CB00022B/833